DEMON PRINCE HADES

LIZA PENN

NATASHA LUXE

PROLOGUE: JOSIE

I smooth down the papers on my lap. Fifty-six pages of meticulously researched analysis of Mount Olympus lore, with more than twenty different works cited, some of them primary sources in the original Ancient Greek. Dr. Phillips had been pretty strict on me, and I get it. She's not just my thesis advisor; she's also got a reputation in the history department. And, well, Greek mythology isn't exactly groundbreaking stuff. It's been a few millennia, but everyone still knows Zeus and Aphrodite and Athena.

But I love it. I love the stories, the history.

The gods and goddesses.

I love them all.

"Josie Granat?" Dr. Phillips calls from her office

without getting up. I stand, take a deep breath, and enter.

Dr. Phillips has books stacked upon books, towering pillars of knowledge that make her small office smell like the best library. I love it here. No candle or perfume could ever capture the scent of paper and ink, of history and stories, the way this room does.

"Josie?" Dr. Phillips says, the hint of annoyance laced with amusement.

"Sorry!" I thrust the papers at her. "My thesis. So far."

Dr. Phillips looks down on it, flipping through the pages. I sit silently, sharing the cracked-leather seat with an old tome so beat-up that I can't even read the title, although I suspect it's not in English.

Dr. Phillips pauses, looking over my works cited pages. "You read Aeschylus?"

"In the original Greek," I say, nodding eagerly.

"And Apuleius."

"I did have to get a little help with the Latin on that one." I lean over, pointing to the translator credited in my thesis.

Dr. Phillips nods absently, but her eyes lose their focus. I bite my lip. If she doesn't approve my thesis work so far, I can't imagine what I could do to ensure I graduate, and—

"This is . . . fine," Dr. Phillips says, interrupting my thoughts.

"Fine?" Not exactly the high praise I was hoping for.

"You can graduate with this." She speaks as if I'd handed her my doctoral thesis proposal written in crayon. "Technically. It's just . . . "

"What?" I cry out when she doesn't finish her train of thought.

"Josie, we've spoken about this before. You excel at research. But no history degree is truly complete without—"

"Boots on the ground," I finish for her, groaning. "But Dr. Phillips, you know I can't afford—"

"I do." She spoke firmly, cutting me off. Dr. Phillips and I had discussed at length how I couldn't afford any international travel. My finances were tight enough just getting through grad school. My mother pays tuition and books, but nothing extra, and I've got too heavy of a course load to work outside of class.

Dr. Phillips pulls out a manilla folder from her top desk drawer and hands it to me. "There's a team that's hiking the Grecian mountains next week. The research assistant originally hired for the job had to back out at the last minute. They need someone to line up the archeological data with the book data. You're perfect."

"But—"

"It's a *paid* position, Josie." Dr. Phillips levels me with a steady look. "Travel, expenses, and a salary."

I swallow, my throat dry.

So.

My excuse about funding won't really work any more.

My hands shake as I look over the contract and additional information in the folder. I have to admit; Dr. Phillips has found basically the *perfect* job for me. Funding taken care of, and the classic "boots on the ground" program that my thesis advisor has been pushing for me to do since I started working with her.

Dr. Phillips's eyes narrow as she watched me. "What's holding you back, Josie?" she asks softly.

You have no idea, I think. But I meet her eyes, biting back my fear. "Nothing," I say firmly, proud that I was able to quash the tremor of fear that would betray me. "Sign me up."

CHAPTER 1
JOSIE

When I said "sign me up," I didn't realize that meant I'd spend the next two hours in Dr. Phillips's office, not only signing the contract to work with the Greek research team, but also buying the international flight tickets for an eye-popping amount. "You have your passport, right?" Dr. Phillips asked me.

I'd nodded mutely, my heart thudding. I'd gotten my passport a few years ago, but I've never used it. It was more of a . . . wishful purchase.

I never thought I actually *could* use it.

But now. . .?

By the time I reach my apartment, my brain is fuzzy with worry and doubt. The papers are crinkled weaty hands.

thing is—this is a *dream* project. It's not just a

great location, but it fits in with my thesis so perfectly it feels as if it were designed for me. A professor—Dr. Reynold, who I've not worked with before—is leading a small group of students, hiking up Mount Olympus and joining a dig at the old temple on the summit previously covered by snow and ice. A heatwave—thanks, global warming—exposed a new area of the ancient temple, and this is a once-in-a-lifetime dig between the weather conditions and permission from the Greek government.

While everyone knows the Greek pantheon lived on Mount Olympus, a lot of people don't realize that not only is Mount Olympus a real place, it's actually really rather accessible. It's not like Everest, where oxygen tanks and years of training are required. The Ancient Greeks put their gods on top of a perfectly accessible mountain.

And that's what the research program is going to cover, that duplicitous nature of a mountain that at once served as home to the gods and also an actual, physical place that anyone could visit. Which lines up with my thesis—on the accessibility of the Greek gods—perfectly.

I fumble my keys, unwilling to relinquish the grip I still have on the manilla envelope with all the paper, including the printed out documents on my newly booked flights.

The door's already unlocked. It swings open with an unexpected creak, and my stomach plunges.

"Josie-baby!" my mother's voice calls from inside, "I'm here!"

Fuck.

I steel myself and step inside my apartment. "Mom," I say, "we discussed this. You can't just come into my apartment on your own."

"Why not?" Mom pokes her head out from the kitchen door. "I pay for the place."

And that's the problem. I'm still reliant upon my mother's funds, and she still believes that her money gives her unfettered access—and control—of my life. And . . . well, I can't really argue with her. My track is so rigorous that it's hard to keep a job, especially since I'm trying to graduate early.

"Are you baking?" I ask, closing the front door behind me and heading to the kitchen. The scent of fresh honey wheat bread wafts through the house.

The thing is, I love my mother. I really do. But she can, at times, be a bit . . . much.

"Of course!" Mom beams at me as she pulls a loaf of bread from the oven. Another loaf—this one loaded down with seeds—is already cooling on a rack. She picks it up, slicing it open and slathering it with butter that melts into the warm bread, drizzling honey on top. I set the manilla folder down and accept the bread, the taste intoxicating.

Sometimes, love for my mother overwhelms me. She raised me alone; not only have I never met my father, I don't even know who he is. Mom doesn't like talking about it. But she's a baker and a giver at heart, and all the best bits of me come from her. She started her bakery-slash-charity, Bountiful Harvest, not only as a way to get income as a single mother, but also as a way to give back to the community; every loaf of homemade bread sold in her bakery funds two loaves donated to all the local shelters and families she knows need a little help.

But as much as Mom has helped the community, she's kept it small. Despite offers for Bountiful Harvest to turn into a franchise, Mom won't sell the brand or her recipes. She's almost paranoid in her secrecy, not even willing to advertise the bakery on Facebook. She didn't want me to come to college, despite it being nearby. It was only when I threatened to leave the state for a different school that she ponied up the cash to pay tuition if I promised to stay local.

"What's this?" Mom's voice is cold, a stark contrast to the buttery bread melting on my tongue. I swallow, eyes widening as Mom pulls out the envelope I'd put on the counter.

"Mom, that's mine," I start, crumbs flying from my lips.

It's too late.

Mom's eyes scan the documents. The flight confirmation. "You're going to *Greece?*" she snarls, all warmth and love gone from her voice.

I cringe. See, Mom's not just paranoid about exposure for the bakery. She's paranoid about either of us leaving the area. Despite the bakery's profits, she's never once taken a vacation. I used to think that it was all about her love of the job and the importance of giving back, but she refuses to even take a day trip out of the city. And she refuses to let *me* go, either.

Class field trips, offers of vacations with friends, family with out-of-town celebrations . . . there ia always an excuse. It's not quite agoraphobia—Mom's fine going anywhere in the city—but it may as well be. If she can't reach it with the subway, it's not a place she'll visit.

Or let me visit.

"Mom, I need to do this for my degree," I say.

"Historians need libraries, not hiking trips," Mom spits back.

"Research can't all be done with books!"

Mom slams the papers back down on the counter. "Is *this* what you're using my money for?" she says.

I shake my head. "It's all paid for. Actually, they're going to pay me."

"Well, I hope they pay you enough for next year's tuition, because if you go on this trip, you can kiss my checks goodbye!"

I gape at Mom. She's always been strict, but . . . "You can't tell me what to do."

Her eyebrows shoot up. "Oh, really? Well, I may not be able to protect you, but I can damn sure make certain you never see a cent of my money."

"Why are you so against this?" I ask. "This is the trip of a lifetime!"

"It's *dangerous!*"

"People fly all the time," I counter. "It's a small mountain, and—"

"You're my daughter! I don't have to give you a reason. You should trust that I know best!" Mom shakes her head in disgust. "And *Greece?!*" She says the country's name as if it were poison on her tongue.

"Give me one good reason not to go," I say quietly.

"Because I'm telling you not to!" There are tears in my mother's eyes. "And you're leaving in a week? How could you do this to me?"

Now there are tears in my eyes, too. I know some of my friends think I'm strange for the way my mom hangs around. She's even crashed some of my study groups, although at least she brought freshly baked cookies. We're close in a way people who aren't raised by a single parent can't really understand.

But I'm starting to realize that she never intended to let me go. Ever.

"Promise me you won't go," Mom pleads. "Promise me. I'll pay the cancellation fees. Just don't go. Don't go where I can't protect you, baby. Please."

"I . . . " I start. My eyes fall on the papers in the manilla folder.

I don't have to go to Greece to write about and study Ancient Greek mythology and literature. I don't have to take Dr. Phillips' advice or her offer.

But I want to.

"Josie," Mom says, her voice cracking over my name. "Baby, please. Don't do this to me. I can't stand the thought of you being half a world away from me."

I nod, but the words she wants to hear won't make their way to my lips. It's enough for her, though, and she wraps me in a hug, certain that my silent nod was a solemn vow.

———

Mom doesn't stick around, thankfully. I take the honey wheat bread she made to Maya's, a Victorian townhouse-turned-café at the edge of campus, and the unofficial home of the Study Group.

There's always some members of the Study Group at Maya's, and today's no different. Cate, Marie, and Sophie are already gathered at the table on the screened-in back porch, mugs of coffee and chocolate in front of them.

"Fresh bread," I say, plunking it down on the table. Maya appears in the doorway. "Get some, too," I offer.

Maya needs no other invitation. She's older than Dr. Phillips, but that just means she's basically a sorority mother to our unofficial sorority, and everyone loves her. We don't use knives, ripping off chunks of bread for each other and eating it plain; Mom's bread is that good.

"You're so lucky," Cate sighs, her eyes crossing in bliss as she inhales the scent of the freshly baked bread.

"Yeah," I mumble.

"Congratulations," Maya says.

"Congratulations?" Marie says. "For what?"

"Dr. Phillips got me a research trip," I say in a low voice.

Sophie whoops with joy as Marie slaps me on the

back. "Yay!" she says.

But Maya has been eyeing me. "What's wrong?"

"My mother," I say, frowning. I look up and realize that all the girls at the table are watching me, concern painted across their features.

I may not have had this university as my top choice, but there's no denying how much I love it. Mom was only willing to pay for me to go to a college in our city, but she had no idea that the Study Group in *this* school was more of a sisterhood than anything else. Nearly every one of us has a different focus—Cate studies South American legends, Marie's specializing in Celtic gods, and Sophie's studying something so obscure I can never keep track of it. What we have in common, though, is that we're all women in men's fields, and we're all either students or advisees under Dr. Phillips. We work together, never in competition.

"So, what's your mom got to do with you going on a research trip?" Cate asks.

I let out a breath. "If I go, she's going to cut off my funding. I won't have her support any more." Shit, I just realized . . . "Or my apartment." Everything's in Mom's name, with Mom's money. And I have no doubt that she will follow through on her threat to cut me off if I don't cooperate with her.

"Why is your mom such a dick?" Marie asks.

"She's not!" I protest. It's . . . complicated with Mom. She's terrified of being abandoned—I suppose because of whoever my father is. And she can't help her phobias.

"You said, 'if' you go . . . " Sophie eyes me.

"When," I say instead. "When I go. Because I am. I am going." Saying it out loud helps. I know it's going to break Mom's heart, but what else can I do? I can't let her hold me back. I know I could get my degree without this trip—as Dr. Phillips said, it would be fine—but I *want* to go.

"That's my girl," Maya says warmly, smiling at the way I roll back my shoulders.

"Besides," Sophie said, "you don't need your mommy's money to go to university. You're a top level doctoral student! I can think of half a dozen grants you can apply for in your last year, to say nothing of the internships that would love to snag you."

Cate leans forward. "Not only that, but your mom doesn't have to know."

"She saw the paperwork."

"And you told her you were going?" Marie knows me too well.

I shake my head. "I may have implied I would do what she wanted."

"So, go. It's for what, two weeks?" Cate asks.

"Three."

"*Go.*" Sophie says, catching on to what my friends are saying. "She may not even notice you're gone."

"She comes to my apartment at least once a week."

"Really?" Cate gapes at me. "She just . . . shows up?"

I nod, miserable.

"That's weird," Marie says.

"It's not!" I protest.

"It is," Cate says gently. "But it's okay. Your mom needs to learn some boundaries. And you need to learn how to take what you want out of life. So you go on your trip. Me and the girls will stop by your apartment every once in a while, make sure it looks lived in. If your mom stops by, we'll say she just missed you, and you're in a class or something."

"It could definitely work," Sophie says, agreeing. "And even if she figures out you're gone, who cares? If she takes back the money, we'll figure out how to make sure you stay in school. We got you."

My stomach clenches at the idea, but I nod, all my doubts evaporating. I can couch surf until I can afford my own place. I can get work—it'll be hard and may delay my degree a little, but I can do it.

I *am* doing this.

I'm going to Greece.

CHAPTER 2
HADES

Hermes is trying to escape.

I sit on the opposite bank of the River Lethe and watch him fumble through the current. He has seen me, I know he has, but the fog of the river's forgetful properties makes it so he does not care, which is reassuring. That holds, at least.

So even though this is his fourth attempt at crossing the River of Forgetfulness to escape his prison in the Underworld, it is nothing to worry about.

Or so my friends continue to tell me.

"He won't make it," says Agapi next to me. They lean forward from where they'd been lounging against a fig tree, reaching for one of the sweetened fruits that's fallen, but their waist-length blonde hair snags in the rough bark, and they flinch with a snarl.

Orfeas frees Agapi's tangles. "Twenty drachmas says he gets to this bank."

Agapi gives their lover a flat look, then grins, all white teeth and red painted lips. "Make it eighty."

"Eighty? Gods, you're confident."

"Bet something else, then, if the price is too rich for you, my dear."

"Hm. Such as?" Orfeas leans in, and the teasing mood shifts abruptly, sharpens into something that for more than a century has never bothered me.

Lately, though, their love is . . . not grating; I am truly happy that they not only found each other, but have stayed together, entirely besotted, long after other demigods would have cast their lovers aside for new blood. They are a rarity not just in the Underworld, in our closed society of god-offspring, but in the whole of the pantheon: true love.

It does not happen for us. It does not happen for gods or any tainted by their blood.

But it happened for Agapi, a descendant of Aphrodite; and Orfeas, a son of Apollo.

It happened. And has held.

And I am so jealous of my two closest friends that it's become a physical ache in my chest.

I stand on the bank, brushing leaves from my black pants. With a wave of my hand, I redirect the currents of the Lethe and send Hermes's form gliding back to the opposite bank. He hits the sand, sputters water, and hauls himself up mechanically, as though his mind is unaware that his limbs are performing the action.

He rises up and turns, staring across the river's flow. At me.

It is not a wide river. Its power, like most things in the Underworld, is not dependent on size. But the distance between this bank and the one he's on feels leagues wide.

Hermes turns, his posture stiff, and as he walks off, back towards the villages clustered throughout that side of the Lethe, he begins to dance, merrily, bouncing to a tune in his head.

Agapi disentangles themself from Orfeas with a chirp. "Ah, see! You lost, my dear. Pay up."

I missed whatever their bet ended up being, but Orfeas groans at me with over dramatic flair. "My lord Hades, you betray me! I am wounded, cut to the quick, utterly devastated—"

"Reinforce this section of the river," I say, hearing the iciness in my voice, unable to stop it. "Around the clock guards, like the others. This cannot keep happening."

That stops Orfeas cold. He rises, Agapi following him up, and they face me, but I'm still angled towards the Lethe, towards that opposite bank, towards the corner of the Underworld where, centuries ago, my ancestor imprisoned himself and many of the other full-blooded gods.

The gods would hate Hades, if they could remember what he did to them. For now, the lot of them—Zeus and Hera and Artemis, Apollo and Hephaestus and Athena, and handfuls of the most vile of their lot—live in a Lethe-induced fog of forgetful bliss, feasting and drinking and fucking each other, living out their god-fantasies on other immortals who are equal to them in power and there-fore able to handle the abuses that inevitably come with a god's appetites.

That is what the instructions my predecessor passed to me explained. Among other things. My duty, as his son and heir, as the next Hades, was to keep these gods imprisoned so as to prevent their rampage of Earth. They had lived in reckless cruelty for too long—and so, the original Hades barred as many gods away as he could lure to this area, at the risk of his own imprisonment, too.

I'm still shocked my father was able to recite such an honorable sentiment to me without choking on his own tongue. But to him, they were just words—to his father, and his father before him, a string of demigods sired by other demigods or, on occasion, mating with the dead mortals who populate the Underworld, all of us leading back to the original, our blood watered down with each passing, but not enough. The demigods here, on this side of the Lethe, are god enough that we are trapped in the Underworld too, but not as severely. We retain our memories, our will, and are able to move about the whole of the Underworld.

Would we know, though, if something had been taken from us? Maybe we're just as blissfully ignorant as Hermes and the other gods.

No. There is nothing *blissful* about our existence.

Agapi touches my shoulder, their fingers curving hard around me. "Of all the gods to attempt passing, it would be clever, mischievous, speedy Hermes. It is nothing to fear."

My jaw sets. "I am not afraid."

I am lonely. I am immensely bored. I am desperate for *anything* new, anything *alive*, to bring brightness and life and *joy* to this oppressive hell.

I am many things.

But I am not afraid.

Even that would be welcome, if only for the novelty of it.

Agapi drops their hand. Out of the corner of my

eye, I see them share a look with Orfeas, an entire unspoken conversation in widening eyes and a lifted brow, and the intimacy of it, of that *connection*, stokes the jealousy I hate that I feel.

"Reinforce this section of river," I say again. I turn, get a few steps, then make myself add, "then pay Agapi their winnings, Orfeas. We keep our word here. What is it they won from you?"

He doesn't miss a beat. "Their cock in my mouth. You can join us, if you like. Since you made me lose— you owe me now, too."

I have joined them before. What else is there to do here? But I haven't since this damned jealousy, since I started to realize exactly how powerful their connection is, and how much I will never find it here.

There are hundreds of demigods in the Underworld. And I know every single one, have bedded many of them, am repulsed by others—so I know, if there was someone down here I could love the way Orfeas and Agapi love each other, I would have found them already. The only new arrivals we get are dead mortals, and I refuse that.

Knowing that I will never get love, and then to be a gloomy third wheel in their fun, is too pathetic a way to spend even a piece of our endless days. We age, but not that quickly.

"Maybe next time," I manage to say, and I leave them on the riverbank, angling onto the road that leads into the demigod city of Elysium.

The river's fig trees quickly cluster with others, a lush tangle of magically enchanted wood that never wilts, never tires, kept alive by similar magic to the Lethe, though these are fed by the River Mnemosyne, one of pure power. The branches curve around the road, and I walk, hands behind my back, my focus grating on the dust in front of me, so I could be surprised by the presence that materializes at the edge of the forest.

But I do not even look up. "What do you want, Zoticus?"

His form emerges from the trees, and I wonder if he sought to startle me. By hiding in shadows, from the reigning king of the Underworld? What an imbecile.

I expect nothing less from a son of Zeus.

Zoticus juts his strong chin back down the road, towards the riverbank. "Hermes failed, I take it?"

"Do you actually care, or did you lose a bet?" Gods, we will need to open a gambling den on the riverbank at this rate. Actually, that may not be a terrible idea, and would ensure that the river stayed guarded, if only by drunk demigods throwing drachmas at each other.

Zoticus's brown skin darkens. He is taller than I am, but I am up on the road, he down by the trees; the high ground is mine, in more ways than one.

Then he speaks. "Your father never had trouble of this sort."

I dig my teeth into the inside of my cheek and force one breath before I respond. "I rejoice in every way I am not like my father. As should you."

Zoticus grunts and steps onto the road. "One day, a Hades will fail us. The Underworld will collapse and all will point and blame your line for what is *imprisonment*, not utopia. And I will be there to watch you crumble."

He is always antagonistic. Always greedy and vengeful that Hades's line rules the demigods, and not Zeus's.

But his words ring too true. They call to the dissatisfaction that poisons my every waking thought.

This is not utopia, despite our calling the city Elysium. This is not utopia, despite my ancestor's vision of a godless world.

This is a cage.

I school my face into impassive disinterest. "It is good to have dreams. Even impossible ones."

Zoticus glowers and starts to walk past me,

towards the river. I continue on opposite him, get a few paces.

"You may not want to go that way," I call without breaking stride, without feeling much of anything beyond my usual ache, now tinged with self-disgust. "Agapi and Orfeas are fucking."

CHAPTER 3
JOSIE

You know that saying, "the real treasure was the friends we made along the way?" Yeah, that does *not* apply to this group. Apparently, the research assistant whose job I replaced had been somewhat beloved. And the team had been together for over two years. They all had their inside jokes and alliances drawn, and I was the bright-eyed naive interloper who took their friend's job, even if I had nothing to do with the friend leaving at the last minute.

They are all nice enough, I guess. It just . . . stings. I'm an afterthought at best. Twice now, I was almost left behind because the group just forgot about me—I made the mistake of going to the bathroom at the airport and the bus almost left without me. Dr. Reynold always seems surprised when I speak up, blinking at me owlishly, with a somewhat baffled expression.

I'm not a hundred percent sure he knows my name. He keeps calling me "Sport," like I'm some British cricket player.

But it doesn't matter.

I'm *here.*

And it's really everything I've ever dreamed of.

Although the tallest mountain in Greece, Mount Olympus is not the tallest mountain in Europe, much less the world. And climbing it's not exactly easy, but it's certainly not treacherous.

Actually . . . it's a tourist attraction. We've passed more than one group that's being led by a Greek guide with a little flag to shepherd the hikers who flew from around the world just to walk the well-beaten trails up the mount. Most people may think of mountain climbers as elite athletes who wear special gear and carry oxygen with them, but this isn't exactly Everest. Don't get me wrong; it's legitimately a hike on an actual mountain. It's just that most people—including me—aren't wearing much more than sturdy shoes and blue jeans for their gear.

Dr. Reynold has us going on the Prionia Trail, which cuts through the Enipea Canyon. It's stunningly gorgeous. This area is a national park, and we're low enough—for now, anyway—that we pass families out for a day trip, little children racing ahead of their parents on the trail.

This is only the first leg of our trip, though—it'll get tougher as we go.

"You sure you can handle it, newbie?" The guy asking me—Josh—is friendly enough, but there's doubt in his voice.

I wipe some sweat out of my eyes, wishing I were more fit. This is what field work is: *work*. And I'm going to do it, even if I sweat my way to the top. "At least it's going to be colder when we reach the summit," I say, shooting him a smile. It's not exactly burning up right now, but the heat wave sweeping Europe does mean that I'm at least a little longing for some snow to roll around in. But, then again, if there hadn't been a heat wave, the second area of the temple wouldn't have been discovered.

"We'll stop at the falls!" Dr. Reynold calls back to the group.

Josh glances at me, and I can see the sympathy in his eyes as I adjust the backpack on my shoulders. As research assistant, my job is to, well, assist. And that means carrying supplies. And *that* means I can't get help now, in the easiest part of the hike, and prove that I was the wrong choice for this mission.

I shoot Josh my best I-got-this smile, and he just

sort of shrugs in response. He doesn't offer to take the pack from me, and for that, I'm grateful.

Even when I start trailing behind some of the others.

To keep my mind off the heat and the weight of the pack, I recite the research program's plans with each step. We started in Litochoro City, after a long bus ride from the airport. We're going up Mount Olympus to Muses Plateau—specifically Stefani Peak, popularly known as Zeus's Throne.

While my job is generally to be the gopher and jack-of-all-trades to help the others, I'm definitely going to find some time to squeeze in the atmosphere of the area. I know the hike isn't exactly easy, but that's not the point. The point is that it's *possible.* And that—the possibility of the average Ancient Greek person to climb the mountain and face the gods personally—is the point of my thesis.

Dr. Phillips was right. This is the type of boots on the ground research I needed all along. I need to take every step of this journey so I know exactly what it must have been like in Ancient Greece. I need to know how it feels to find the drive to make this climb.

To face the gods.

And to realize they aren't there.

Sweat stings my eyes, and I heft the bag on my

shoulders again. It's heavier than I had anticipated. Everyone else on this trip has trained for this hike, mentally and physically. I'm fit, but I'm not carry-the-extra-trowels-up-a-mountain fit.

Without meaning to, I've fallen a little behind the others. I pick up my pace, the steel instruments clanging together in my pack. By the time I follow the trail past the historic monastery, over the wooden bridge, and to the Enipea Falls, everyone else is already there, eating a snack.

"Oh! Joan! Welcome, welcome!" Dr. Reynold calls to me, waving an orange in my direction.

"It's Josie," I say. I grab a banana and collapse on the ground.

Dr. Reynold checks his watch. "We were about to . . ." He casts his eyes over me. "Actually, I think a little bit of a longer break is warranted."

Great. I'm already slowing the group down. They were just about to leave this area by the time I got here.

"A longer break?" Romilla, another doctoral student, says. "Then I'm going in."

She had already taken her boots off, but as I watch, she strips off her sweaty t-shirt and walks out into the pool of water near the falls in her sports bra and leggings. Romilla groans in pleasure as the cool water sloshes to her knees. "C'mon in! It's great!"

"You don't have to tell me twice," Josh says, stripping to his boxers and splashing in.

Dr. Reynold seems more amused than frustrated, and I down the banana, then follow Romilla's lead. I was wearing jeans, but I have biker shorts under them, so it's not that hard for me to get to a point where I can swim into the falls. I go further out than the others, swimming closer to the short waterfalls, slipping behind them so I can wet my whole body. I don't care that I'll have to walk a while with wet hair and wet underwear. This moment is totally worth it.

Three more hours, I tell myself, the water cascading over my body. That'll get us to the Spilios Agapitos Refuge, where we'll spend the night. I can do three more hours. The next day will be harder, heading toward Mytikas. But after that? We'll be there.

A real archeological dig of an ancient Greek temple. Dr. Reynold said that on a clear day, we'll be able to see all the way to Bulgaria or Albania, but my eyes will be down, on the ground that the Ancient Greeks walked on, knelt on.

Through the cascading falls, I can hear Romilla and Josh goofing off, playing. Someone else calls out. It's probably time to go.

I shut my eyes. This? This is worth the threat of losing my mother's support, financial or otherwise. This is worth the long flight, the hard walk.

This is everything I ever dreamed of.

"I'm going to find the gods," I whisper to the water.

My stomach lurches. My breath catches.

"Is that everyone? Someone get the spare pack!" Dr. Reynold calls out, his voice carrying. Spare pack? No—that's *my* pack. Has he already forgotten about me again?

The water feels heavy, like it's trying to pull me under. My brain is fuzzy. Perhaps it wasn't a good idea to go from hot, arid air to cool water.

I try to focus even as my eyes blur. I hope this isn't a heat stroke.

A dead leaf drifts behind the waterfall. I watch its crisp, curled edges, and I reach out to touch it.

It bursts into color—vivid green, shiny and strong.

"What is happening?" I ask, but my voice sounds distant even to myself. As if I'm moving in slow motion, I turn my head and see the research group heading out.

Without me.

I raise my hand. I think I shout—*Wait!*--but I'm not sure any sound leaves me.

A tug at my navel.

Behind the waterfall there is stone, solid earth.

But I fall through it, disappearing into the dark.

CHAPTER 4
HADES

lounge back on my onyx throne and stare through the supplicant before me. Some descendant of Poseidon, I think; I don't remember what Agapi said when they announced the next speaker. I should know. I should care. Whoever he is, he's going on about a string of robberies in a neighborhood on the eastern side of Elysium.

I lean forward, elbows on my knees, trying hard to focus on the demigod's pleading face.

"There are no suspects?" I clarify, cutting him off from his repetition of the story.

He shakes his head.

"Local guards have been ineffective?"

A nod.

I glance up at Agapi, next to me, who gives a quick eye roll. It's all I need to know.

The neighborhood falls under Zoticus's guard. Of course.

Do I dare piss him off more by taking the position away from him? This is not the first time responsibilities under his domain have fallen short.

If I do take this from him, he will retaliate.

And for a moment, the spark of interest lights within me.

His retaliation would be violent and cruel and—and *interesting*. Something to do. Something *different*, mildly, but still *something*, and I could have enough cause to beat the living shit out of him.

I run my thumb along my jaw, thinking, then look up at Agapi again. "Summon Zoticus."

A tug in my chest might be caution, but I am too consumed with this new focus. A way to expel this tangle of toxic energy on someone who deserves this negativity, who deserves my wrath.

He may have just handed me exactly what I need.

Agapi leaves a moment, returns with quick, frantic steps. "My lord—Zoticus is . . ." They flip a look at the waiting descendant of Poseidon, then lower their voice. "Not at his post."

And I am not even surprised.

I stand, dismiss the supplicant with a hand wave, and as a servant ushers them out, clearing the throne room, I frown at Agapi's tighter-than-usual discomfort.

"Then let us go and find him, shall we?" I give a grin that is in no way joyous, and Agapi's discomfort deepens. "This is a proclamation I will deliver in person."

Agapi puts their hand out when I take a step forward. "What is with you lately?"

Their drop of formality in the absence of anyone else shakes through me, feeling mildly like a child being scolded. "Nothing. I have business to attend."

"I do not like this energy coming from you," they say. "You cannot antagonize Zoticus."

"I am not. I am exacting consequences to his own actions, as a king should."

"Are you? Or are you looking for a punching bag?"

My face falls, briefly, but Agapi catches it.

They roll their eyes again. "Shit, Hades. You're better than this. Do not go dragging us into a war because you're bored. You have no shortage of people to fuck. Stick your cock in something *before* you plant your fist in someone's face."

It is not that simple. It is not that *fucking* simple, and the fact that they try to boil it down to just a place to stick my cock is infuriating.

I suck my teeth. "Should you really speak to your king this way?"

"No. I'm speaking to my asshole of a friend this way." Agapi pats my cheek and gives me a feline smile. "Need me to arrange some lovers for you? I have a skill at—"

The doors at the end of the throne room slam open.

I exhale a sigh of relief to be saved from this conversation—

And when I turn, that relief piques even higher.

Orfeas and his guards are dragging Zoticus towards me, his arms shackled in enchanted chains.

Good. *Good.* Agapi can hardly be against me doling out punishment when Zoticus has clearly been caught doing—something. My mind trips. Orfeas wouldn't have needed to chain him just for abandoning his post, and I have given no proclamation of Zoticus being stripped of his responsibilities yet.

So Zoticus was caught doing something that earned his imprisonment.

Molten joy bubbles in my stomach, and I'm halfway down the throne's dais before I register the other being the guards have in their clutches.

An unconscious woman.

An unconscious *human* woman. Not a shade or a ghost, but a living, breathing human.

I stop. Fully rigid, hands splayed at my sides.

She is unmistakably human. The smell of her on the air, a scent like honey and flower blossoms and—and something else, something I recognize, and I sniff again, and throw a furious glower at Orfeas, who stops at the base of the dais.

He shoves Zoticus to his knees before me. "Caught him at the inlet of the River Mnemosyne, abducting a human."

Hot, liquid rage floods my body. I can feel my powers sparking to life, little flickers of flame in my dark eyes that I fix on Zoticus, who looks up at me, unafraid.

Stupid, pathetic demigod.

"You abducted a *human*?" My chest heaves, and I pivot that glare to Orfeas. "Why did you bring her here? Return her to the—"

I stop. Because the air smells of her so strongly, so potently, that my own question is answered.

She is not just human.

She is one of us. A demigod. And not merely a fraction, but so strongly humming with god blood that she must be close to a direct descendant, which is not only unlikely, but *impossible*.

My rage falls to a simmer against the sharp,

breathless rise of curiosity. I do not let it show on my face. I will not.

I take another step down the dais. Zoticus growls.

"She's not a human," he says, as though I have not realized. "She's one of us. I saw her use powers in the water. She turned a dead leaf green again. She's—"

"You went beyond our borders."

"I never left our realm. I was in the river the whole time. You have nothing on me. I found her, she's *mine*, and I don't appreciate things that are rightfully mine being stolen from me!" His words bellow out, but I am unfazed.

I close the distance between us and punch him in the face.

His head throws to the side, blood spraying across the floor from the immediate burst of his nose. He tries to scramble to his feet, to fight back, but Orfeas and another guard hold him easily.

I crouch down, into his face. "You walk too fine a line, Zoticus. You do not leave the Underworld. Semantics of boundaries in river water will not save you. And we do not abduct our own, or any, in fact, but you do not lay claim to an *unconscious demigod*. Following too boldly in your ancestor's footsteps. Should I punish you as he is? I would do well to be rid of you entirely, let the River Lethe cleanse you of your pomposity and useless pride."

Zoticus spits blood at me. I let it hit my cheek, eyes shutting once.

Then I punch him again.

Gods, it feels good.

My knuckles burn as I straighten. "Lock him in the dungeon."

"You *cannot*—" he starts, but guards immediately drag him back, and he falters, slipping to his feet, spitting curses and writhing.

Orfeas remains, Agapi rushing down to my side, and I turn to the two remaining guards holding the unconscious mortal—demigod—between them.

I step closer.

Then stop.

As though I have hit a wall. As though there is a force around her that has turned my body to marble.

She is drenched, a clear mark of the river, in the sort of clothing that dead mortals have been coming here wearing in recent years. Tight shorts, a tight green bra pressing her small breasts flat. Her hair is a tangled mess of deep blonde, heavy with water, darkened as it falls across her cheeks, her sun-browned skin showing freckles across her face, her shoulders, her bare stomach—

The smell of her on the air is even stronger.

Honey and flower blossoms and that electric charge of demigod power, and it all goes straight to my growing cock.

She is achingly beautiful. Truly, achingly, in a way that yanks the air from my lungs and leaves me feeling as though Zoticus returned a blow to my gut. I'm overwhelmed with the sudden urge to demand these guards *put her down*, how dare they touch her like this? But she is wet and unconscious and must be freezing, and when she wakes up, she will be terrified—

My jaw sets. "She is from Earth?"

Orfeas nods. "She's a demigod, but we have no record of her."

All demigods and any of god blood are required to stay in the Underworld. It was the original Hades' proclamation. We have separated ourselves from the mortal world. We are done with it.

There are a few who slipped through his grasp, though. A small handful of gods who did not fall for his ploy to ensnare them, and over the centuries, they have never caused trouble on Earth. My predecessors tried to track them down, of course, as best we could with only the most trusted excursions to Earth to search. There have only been one or two cases of new demigods created on Earth, and they were immediately brought to the Underworld.

So this. Her.

She is inconceivable.

Rare.

New.

Part of me waits for the punch of happiness at this, at something new when I had been wanting such a thing for so long.

But all I feel, staring down at her, is rage. Manic, furious rage.

That she was on Earth, when she should have been here all along.

That she was abducted, no doubt violently, by Zoticus, and if he harmed her, *touched* her, in anyway

. . .

That she is here now, and when she wakes up, she will be terrified and angry and no doubt want to go home.

And I cannot let her do that. Not now that she is here. It is the law of my ancestor—even a drop of immortal blood means she must spend the rest of her life in the Underworld.

She will undoubtedly hate that, and there is nothing in my vast power I can do to ease this transition.

Except—

"Have her moved to a chamber in my wing," I say to Agapi, my eyes on the new demigod. "Have her cared for, cleaned, given new clothing. Let me know the *moment* she wakes up—no one is to speak to her before I do. Understand?"

Agapi is watching me strangely. Their eyes slant, lips set to the side.

But they nod. "Of course."

They walk away, leading the guards out, and I almost snarl at them to be gentle with her.

Orfeas remains. Watching me with a look that matches his lover's speculation.

"If you have a thought, share it," I snap.

He huffs. "Merely that your wishes may have been answered."

It shakes me back, and I fold my arms before realizing how defensive that is.

I can't help but ask, voice low, rumbling, "Am I that transparent?"

Orfeas pulses an eyebrow. "To those who know you. And you know nothing of her yet, so restrain whatever thoughts you are having until she is awake."

"If you think for one moment that I would have any of the same inclinations as Zoticus—"

"That is not at all what I think. I think you have slowly been falling into more and more of a desperate state, Hades, and the way you looked at her was the way Agapi looks when they talk about seeing the sun again."

It is a double-edged sword, those words. That we will never see the sun again.

That Orfeas saw right through me.

"I will handle it," I tell him, because there is no other choice.

I am the king of the Underworld.

And I will not be rocked by a single demigod. No matter how much my body—my soul—already longs for her.

CHAPTER 5
JOSIE

My body is deeply still, and even as my mind awakens, I keep myself motionless, coming into awareness without opening my eyes. My muscles ache, and I know that if I move, they will scream in protest. Best to lie still.

I was hiking, an activity I had *thought* I was prepared for but clearly am not as fit as I once thought. I remember . . .

The waterfalls.

The cool pool of water.

A leaf, shifting from dead to alive again.

No, that part is impossible. It must have been a dream.

I probe my mind, trying to figure out the rest of the events. I should have gotten the pack by the pool, I should have gone with the group to the refuge up the path. I should be in a bed worn from use, the hostel-like refuge designed for service, not comfort. But the bed I'm in is luxuriously soft, the cover over me like silk, the air fragrant with citrus blossoms. And I have no memory of being here.

My eyes fly open, and I shoot up in the bed, my hand sinking into the feather down mattress. Gauzy white drapes cover the bed, hung from the ceiling, but there is an ethereal light floating through them. A draft causes them to stir, a shadow beyond shifting.

As I watch, I see the shadow more clearly. It looks like . . .

A man.

Trembling, I glance down at myself. Diaphanous white robes *barely* cover my body, and there's no underwear in sight.

What the fuck happened to me?

And there's a man on the other side of this almost see-through curtain, and while I can't see him distinctly, I can tell that he's watching me.

I should be terrified. I don't remember how I got here—I don't remember anything after the falls—and I don't know how I came to be in these robes, in this room, on this bed. And whoever is watching me—*he* must know. He must have done something. To me. I should be terrified.

I'm not.

I'm pissed right the fuck off.

I thrust my arm through an opening in the gauzy white curtains and fling them aside so violently that the man on the other side startles in the chair he'd been sitting in, his dark eyes widening ever so slightly.

And—oh, fuck.

He's *hot*.

My rage is tempered momentarily by the sheer fuckability of this dude. I mean—he's got a broad chest that looks rock hard, black hair rakishly long just begging for my fingers to tousle it more, and eyes that are as intense as a raging inferno. I could get lost in those eyes. I, uh, I *do* get lost in those eyes.

Suddenly, I remember myself, my situation. Hot or not, I'm not forgiving him if he's kidnapped me. I clutch the thin, white fabric of the robes at my chest. "What the fuck is going on?" I snarl. And then, because he does nothing more than widen those big, dark eyes of his, I switch to Greek, since I don't think I've been taken out of the country, at least.

"You are safe now," he answers in Greek, his accent sweet as baklava.

"That means I wasn't safe before. What happened?"

He's got a calmness to him that I appreciate, something that immediately mellows me. "You were taken. Not by me. The person who kidnapped you is being punished." He practically growls those last words.

"But—my clothes?" I say, hating the tremor in my voice. "Where am I?"

"That is . . . " For the first time, the man looks uneasy, and I'm back on edge, a bundle of rage and nerves. "That is a complicated situation."

"What the fuck is complicated about telling me where I am?" I snarl, looking around the room. Tile mosaic covers the floor, the repeated design classic Greek. There's a fireplace in one wall, the crackling flames adding a gentle warmth.

We were in the middle of a heat wave, I remind myself. I shouldn't be somewhere where a fire is needed. Unless perhaps I'm further up the mountain than I thought? I wouldn't mind that—I don't relish the idea of being kidnapped, but if I could avoid the hike up Mount Olympus . . .

I scan the room, looking for windows. The view outside will give me a clue.

There are no windows.

There's one door, and the man is blocking it.

His broad shoulders and heavy muscles no longer seem so hot. Not if he's keeping me captive. And this place is feeling far too confined for comfort.

"Are you keeping me prisoner?" I ask, my eyes flicking over his shoulder to the door.

The man flinches.

Not a good sign.

"What the fuck is going on?" I ask, my heartbeat in my throat.

"I can tell you, but it'll be easier to show you."

If it gets me out of this room, which is feeling more claustrophobic by the minute . . . "Okay."

The man stands. He's taller than I thought, and he moves with a distinct, feline, feral smoothness, like a big cat stalking its prey. But when he opens the door and turns to me with a smile, his teeth perfectly white, my knees melt.

I shake myself. "Who are you?" I ask, glad that my voice is demanding and without a quiver, despite my treacherous, wet pussy that is practically purring in anticipation.

"I am the . . . ruler of this area."

"Ruler?" I lift my eyebrow. "Like a king?"

"Like one."

Well, that's strange as fuck. I'm starting to think I may not be in Greece any more. I glance down the hallway, broad marble light and airy, but despite the columns along the corridor, there are—again—no windows.

And no other people. Apparently this dude is

powerful enough to command a mansion without interruption. The corridor is long, with rooms branching off to the sides, but there's a clear destination in mind; the end of the hall leads to a wide, open staircase and, presumably, outside.

"Okay, but what do I call you?" I ask.

He hesitates. Maybe he's going to lie. He looks down at me, and he doesn't seem like he's going to lie to me, but I can't get a bead on him. "Hades," he answers finally.

"Hades," I repeat flatly. "Cool, okay. My name is Persephone then."

"Really?" That stops him cold, his face painted with shock.

"No, idiot, my name is Josie."

"Oh." He's a little disappointed, which is weird, but at least I see a flicker of a smile at my joke.

"Fine, 'Hades,'" I say, unable to take the name seriously. "Where are we? In Greece?"

"Er," he says, stalling, without giving me an answer. He leads me to a set of beautifully cut marble stairs. I see more people as we step outside on the wide space before the stairs descend outside. I pause at the top of the steps, looking out and around.

There's no sky.

We're in a cave of some sort, some vast, underground network. I can see reddish brown rock high above us, but I'm not sure where the light is coming from. And even if this is a cave, it's bigger than any cave I've ever seen—big enough for a whole city to be built here, all in the classical Ancient Greek architecture.

"We are in the Underworld," Hades says.

I feel myself dissociating. He's . . . Hades? Like, the Greek god Hades? I wouldn't have believed it—I didn't believe it five minutes ago—but this *is* some sort of Underworld, there's no denying that. It's . . . I mean, it's a whole city in a cave. A classic Greek city.

"Josie?" Hades asks gently.

Ancient Greeks were pretty damn literal when it came to gods. Zeus and the whole pantheon were basically immortal humans, fucking around, usually literally, and acting like fallible, stupid humans that happened to have powers and lived on top of the very literal and reachable mountain, Olympus. The Underworld, the realm of Hades, was supposed to be a literal, actual cave under the ground, and there are a few theories as to which one it was, but this?

This is next level.

"Josie, come with me," Hades says when I don't move. He slips his big, warm hand in mine and pulls me gently down the stairs. My mouth is agape as I trail beside him, down a hill and toward the rivers.

I can see glittering rivers cutting through the city

from this vantage point. One, further away, acts seemingly like a barrier. One is much closer. Hades brings me to the closer one.

"This is River Mnemosyne," Hades says as we draw near its banks. "It will—"

"Am I dead?" I ask hollowly.

"What?" Hades looks genuinely shocked. "No, of course not."

"I mean, if I am dead, it's kind of nice to know that at least some version of an afterlife exists. Huh. So it was the Greeks all along."

"You're *not* dead," Hades says. He grips my shoulder, shifting my view to the river slightly further away, but still easily accessible. The bank on the far shore is no more than a city block away, the rivers not quite converging, but remarkably close. "That's a dead soul."

His words make me expect to see a ghost, but while the person Hades shows me is . . . not a person, not any more . . . it's also unlike anything I could have described.

I went to Madame Tussauds once, a tourist trap of wax works, and this shade reminds me of that—not that it looks like a wax statue of a person, but it has that same eerie almost-but-not-quite-right uncanny valley thing going on.

I look down at my hands. They look like my hands. Living hands.

"You're not dead," Hades says again, gentler this time.

I nod mutely. "Then why am I here?" I ask when he does nothing more than stare at me with those huge, dark eyes of his. "This is the Ancient Greek Underworld, right?"

"Yes."

"You're Hades."

"Yes."

"I'm not dead."

"Yes."

"A living human is not supposed to be here," I say, frustrated. Not according to any of the legends. And while the people on this side of the river are keeping their distance from Hades and me, they seem . . . *more* than me, too, like they're . . .

Oh my god, they're gods.

"Humans aren't supposed to be here," I continue.

"Yes," Hades says, but there's a different cadence to his tone. He's not just agreeing with me . . . he's trying to get me to understand something. "I need you to drink from the River Mnemosyne. It has powers."

"Yes, I know," I say. "Mnemosyne grants its

drinkers memory, while Lethe makes you forget things."

"It's not as simple as that," Hades says. "Mnemosyne gives knowledge; Lethe gives ignorance."

I narrow my eyes at him. Confusion crosses his face. "Why do you hesitate?" he asks. "You wanted knowledge; the river gives it."

I let out a shaky breath. I know this—at least according to legends. The Greek mythology was pretty clear on how River Mnemosyne was reserved for the dead who wished to relive the memories of the past, a blessing to the heroes who got to revel in the replays of their greatest hits. It stands to reason that what Hades is offering is real.

Except what the fuck, no it doesn't, there's no *reason* here at all. It's Greek *mythology*, not reality. And besides, what about the other legends, the ones that tricked mortals like me into traps. Orpheus looking back as he escaped the Underworld and losing his shot at saving his love by a technicality. Persephone being trapped in the Underworld for part of each year based on how many pomegranate seeds she had eaten. Poor dead souls unable to cross the River Styx because they didn't have coins to pay the ferryman.

If there's one thing Greek mythology has taught

me, it's that there's a price to be paid for *everything* that happens down here.

Hades leans down, peering into my eyes. "I promise you," he says, as if he can read my worried mind, "drinking from this river will only give you the truth. It may give you more truth than you want, but it will still be true. It is knowledge only."

I hesitate.

"Trust me," he says, his voice liquid.

And by all the gods of any pantheon, I cannot help crumple at the cadence of his voice. I do. I trust him. And besides, I could certainly use some knowledge. I kneel at the bank of the river. Its waters look just like regular water, but I don't need Hades and the Underworld to remind me that it's not. I cup my hands and dip them into the cool, gently flowing river. Crystal clear water pools in my palms. I bring the water to my lips, take a sip and—

My senses *explode* in cacophonous chaos.

I *know*—without really understanding how I know—that my mother is *Demeter, goddess of the fucking harvest.* She's an immortal being who knew Zeus himself, Kronos, all the old gods. She escaped because, unlike the others, she never really cared for Mount Olympus. She lived on Earth, hidden among mortals, a benevolent force, albeit in hiding.

And at the same time I come to know this, I also become aware of other knowledge:

This Hades is not the original Hades.

But the original Hades saw, long ago, just how cruel and meddlesome the gods were.

So he decided to restrain them.

He used the waters of Lethe to make them forget their former lives of fucking around with humans and making a mess of everything.

And he slowly, carefully, drew the net around every god and goddess . . .

. . . and their children, the demigods.

Children like me.

Grief and fear and terror and *rage* course through me, everything all at once. I feel so much that I think I'm going to explode—distantly, I'm aware that something, at least, actually *is* exploding. Vivid yellow and purple and pink and red and green bursts around me, colors too bright for this dark Underworld, but they only add to the chaos raging inside of me, outside of me, everywhere, everywhere, everywhere.

CHAPTER 6
HADES

On the bank of the Mnemosyne, Josie is creating a forest.

For a moment, I stand there, watching her, stricken by the potency of her abilities.

We have plant life here, but it is sad, a mockery of what truly exists above the surface. Every leaf and blade of grass is created via magic, drawn from art and descriptions in long-aged scrolls and books.

But what Josie is creating is *real*.

The air is saturated with the sharp floral tang of pollen and greenery, flowers and vines rippling out from the apex that is her body where she kneels down, hands on the river's edge, shoulders shaking.

It's that shake, the tremble, that grabs me and drives me forward. Behind me, toward the palace, I hear cries of alarm as others see the sudden onslaught of plant life—life, new and green and growing in this place that is only the same—and I take hold of Josie's arms and pull her to her feet.

She goes limp, and the moment her hands release from the ground, the explosion of plant life stops. We are in a nest of rainbow petals and snarled vines now, concentric circles of plants spiraling out around us, and I hold her up when I feel her weight start to sag. She is small, so slender I could bundle her into my arms easily, but I want to see her face.

"Josie," I say her name, unintentionally taking care over each letter. "What did you see?"

I know, though.

I can feel it in her. I can smell it, taste it on the air.

There are only a few gods who escaped my ancestor.

Demeter is one.

We have not heard from her, much less one of her descendants, since Hades ensnared the other gods. I did not even think she *had* descendants, and had honestly begun to wonder if she was even on Earth at all anymore.

But I am holding one of her daughters in my hands, staring down into hazel eyes rimmed with visceral anger—and the smallest, most heartbreaking flicker of betrayal.

"She knew," Josie says, and it comes out as a

whimper that breaks her rage, letting only the betrayal through. "My mother. She knew the whole time—I'm a *god?*"

"Demigod," I clarify.

"That isn't any less shitty!"

"Josie." Her outburst sent a spray of ferns covering the ground at our feet. We have an audience now, others wandering out of the palace, staying a good few yards back from the edge of the vine and flower swirls she's made, but watching all the same.

Agapi is there, their eyes wide.

"You are a descendant of the goddess of the harvest," I say. "Of plants and agriculture. You—"

"*I fucking am not!*"

Another surge of plants, this one snarled, vicious thorned trunks that launch from the ground, all but caging us in.

I do not flinch. Do not react.

"Josie," I say her name harder, demanding, the tone of my throne room, of unarguable authority. "Breathe. Now."

She glares at me. Shaking in my grip, but that glare is rage, not fear or brokenness, so I pinch my hands on her arms and pull her closer, cocooning her in the circle of my arms. I am acting on instinct and do not realize until I have her against my chest that she may not want it, but her tension immediately goes out more, whether she's conscious of it or not.

I hold her tighter. Closer. My lips fall to her ear, brushing the soft curls of hair over her cheek.

"You were lied to. By your mother. She did not tell you what you are?" It is a guess and a question.

She whimpers. More thorns sprout on the branches, growing, arching towards us, towards *her*—

"You are the descendant of a goddess, Josie," I tell her. She trembles against me, her fingers rising up to hold onto my back, digging into my spine. "You were lied to, but you know the truth now, and you have every right to rage, but I will not let you harm your-self in that destruction."

I peel back to meet her eyes, hand cupping her jaw.

"Do you—look at me, Josie."

Her eyes snap up to mine in a startled pull, and for the first time, I see clarity break through, or at least her focus drawing elsewhere. To me.

And the full brunt of her attention floods my body as though she sprouted life and greenery in my veins, all of it racing towards my cock.

"You see the thorns you have made?" I ask, voice perfectly level, though I am on the edge of panic. If I cannot get her to calm down . . . "You *will not* hurt yourself with them. I won't let you. Stop, now, and breathe. I will guide you as you deserve and answer any questions you have. Can you allow me to do that, Josie? Can you trust me to know what you need for now?"

She sucks in a breath, staring at me, watery eyes shifting through mine in the poked shadows of the thorny branches surrounding us.

"Answer me," I command.

She nods. "Yes." It bursts out of her, small and desperate, and I feel some of her tension start to go out.

She is relaxing in what I am offering, however unconsciously.

I chase that feeling. Knowing that her stress is leaving, that she is letting me take some of that burden, that I can, in this way, help her.

"You are under my protection here," I say. "In every way. You will not fear or worry. Do you understand, Josie? I will keep you safe."

"Why?" It's a whisper. A beg.

The roll of her lips, the pleading look in her eye —my already hard cock strains against my pants, and I hold her arms now to brace myself, not just her.

I imagine her lips parting like that, but saying other words. *Please,* and *More,* and even *Fuck me.*

My eyelids flutter shut, breath heaving, steadying.

I open my eyes when I am composed.

"Because you are mine." The words come, unbidden. Was that too forward? But it is the truth—her being a demigod, officially, but deeper than that is what I truly mean. The expansiveness of her presence here is a whirlwind, and I am swept up into her.

But she does not seem put off by my statement.

If anything, the softening of her face pinches, eyebrows bending sharply up.

And then she shoves into me, arms throwing around my neck, and kisses me.

CHAPTER 7
JOSIE

t's because he says to trust him like he means it with his whole heart, like he would die rather than break my faith.

It's because I always knew my mother, the person closest to me, was hiding *something*, but this man is an open book, his eyes begging me to ask anything just so he can reveal more truths.

It's because when he gives me an order, his voice cuts right into the core of me, my soul singing out that it *wants* to obey.

It's all these things and more; it's lust, it's want, it's desire, it's *everything*. And while my mind is in chaotic turmoil to discover that all my past has been a lie, everything I knew about myself untrue, *he* is standing in the center of the storm, strong and stalwart and steady.

I pull back from the kiss, breathless, searching his eyes. "I'm sorry," I whisper.

"What for?" His voice is low and gravelly, almost a growl.

I let my head fall on his hard chest, but I have my eyes open now, clearly seeing the snarling, twisting plants that sprang up around us at the river's edge. "I'm sorry I lost control," I whisper. "In more ways than one."

He pulls me gently back, his gaze soft with sympathy. "Never apologize to me," he says. "You are a new demigod, new to your powers. You only lost control because you've had no one to guide you. Your powers have remained dormant, but now . . . "

"Hades!" a voice calls from the other side of the brambles. The thorns and plants are so thick that I can barely see the people beyond, but a crowd has gathered. "Are you okay? Erastus, fetch some blades to cut this down!"

I shrink against Hades. I feel safe here, with him, but out there?

His arms tighten against me. "I am fine!" he shouts back, his voice commanding in a way that makes my body clench with pleasure.

"But—" The voice this time sounds female, but I'm not sure.

"We have discovered not only the presence of

Demeter, a lost goddess on Earth, but her offspring," Hades says, his voice rumbling over my head as his arms hold me against his chest. "I shall discuss more with the daughter. Alone."

The others stop attacking the plants.

"Meanwhile," Hades continues, "gather the council."

My stomach drops at that—is he gathering the council to discuss my mother? A "lost" goddess? But before I can think too much on that, I hear the people—or, demigods, I suppose—dispersing beyond my plant barrier as they obey Hades's command.

"Everyone obeys you," I say, unwilling to admit even to myself how much of a turn on that is. I never really explored much—it's hard to get it on when you live with your mother or when she can show up at your apartment at any point in time—but I'm quite liking this discovery of how wet authority like his makes me.

Hades hesitates. "Everyone is supposed to obey me," he mutters.

I look past him, squinting through the plants that I made erupt from the ground, caging us in. "I think we're alone."

"We are," he says, his voice dropping. His eyes are liquid, feral, watching me.

"What . . . " I bite my lip. "What were you going to discuss with me?"

"Do you think you have control over your powers now?"

I close my eyes, feeling for the plants. I've always liked plants well enough, but I never really *felt* them like this. A connection, a link between me and them, coming as easily to me as breathing. "I think I can lower the walls," I say. I reach for the tangle of thorns in my mind, and the plants start to recede.

"Wait." Hades touches my arm, and a crown of bright red roses bursts over the plant cage I've made, their sweet scent cascading around us. Hades doesn't hide his smile. "I only mean . . . we could do with privacy."

"Oh." My heart thumps. He can't mean like . . . he can't want privacy for *that* . . . But even as I think it, more vivid red blossoms bloom all around us, filling every tiny crevice between the thorns until it really is like we're in a private botanical bubble.

Hades's eyes slowly move from blossom to blossom until his gaze rests fully on me. "Beautiful," he says, his voice low and warm. He takes a step closer to me. "You're calm now." It's a statement, not a question. "You're in control."

I nod once, silently.

He's close enough that I can smell the scent of

him—smoke and musk mingling with the floral perfume in the air. His thick finger trails along my cheek bone, catching a stray lock of hair and tucking it behind my ear. His touch is hot against my skin, and a thin line of a honeysuckle vine trickles over my cheek, emerging from air and dropping between us when he pulls his hand away from me.

"I'm in control thanks to you," I say softly, remembering the way my panic made a garden burst from the dry soil.

Hades shakes his head. "You have the power; I only reminded you of it."

Perhaps I like the way you remind me of power, I think, my heart beating louder, but I don't say the words out loud. The heady scent of the roses feels heavier now, intoxicating. I meet his eyes, but I cannot read the expression in their darkness. So *broody* this man, but that's coming from a place of barely-checked power within him and that? That's driving me wild.

This—all of it, the new knowledge of my mother's godhood, my powers, *him*—all of it hits me, all at once, and the panic flares over me again. How can any of this be real? More blooms burst around us, pushing us closer and closer together.

"Josie?" Hades asks.

"I don't have power, or—I do—but I can't control

it!" I sob. The perfumed scent of the flowers is making me dizzy. I feel at once my own panic, but also I can sense the flowers, the plants. They want to comfort me, but that knowledge just makes my hysteria rise.

"What can I do to help?" Hades asks, his voice cutting through my fear.

I think about what he did before, when I first called the flowers. His touch grounded me. Without thinking, I reach out and grab him arm. He responds immediately, using his other hand to grip my shoulder and pull me against his firm chest.

The flowers stop erupting in blooms everywhere.

"You're okay," Hades says. "I'll talk you thought this, but you're going to lower these vines with your own power. And you're going to be in control."

The way he talks does something to me. His voice is calm, but also firm. "I like the way you give me commands," I murmur against his chest, the words slipping out of me before I can censor myself. I'm glad he's holding me tightly; he can't see the blush that stains my cheeks.

My ear is pressed against his chest, so I hear the low chuckle deep in his throat reverberating through him.

"What command would you like me to give?" he asks.

I want you to lick me until I scream, I think, but I can't say that, I shouldn't even be thinking it. I let out a shaky breath, trying to focus, trying to figure out just what it is that I need to focus on so I can lower the plants and get us out of this private oasis in the middle of the Underworld, except . . .

I don't want to get us out of this little bubble made of flowers and vines.

And my powers know that, even if my mind won't admit it.

The vines work my will, snaking down and wrapping Hades closer to me. I feel safe in his arms, and the plants know it, and they want to make sure we're together.

Hades chuckles again. He's had experience with demigods' powers, I assume. "You want something, I take it?"

I can't, I can't—I'm just a regular girl, a university student focused on her doctorate; I was hiking for a research program, goddammit, I don't . . . I can't . . .

But the vines tug his hands down my back, gently, pushing him to do what I want him to do even if I can't wrap my head around the reality of *any* of this.

Hades looks down at me. "We are alone, demigoddess. Your plants have seen to that. And you need to remind them that *you* are in control, not them."

I am in control.

And the vines are swirling around us *because* I am in control.

And I want this.

I lean up and kiss him on the lips again. "I am in control," I say, repeating my thoughts, making them real. "And we are alone. And maybe . . . "

"You're playing with fire," Hades says, a wicked glint in his eyes.

"Good." I kiss him again, and this time, his hands grip my body, clutching at me like his desire will kill him if he doesn't respond. With a growl, Hades drops to his knees in front of me, grabs my hips, and pulls me closer.

The gauzy white robes someone dressed me seem designed for easy access, and while the cloth has been wrapping around my legs in diaphanous waves as I walked, Hades parts it easily. His hands slide over my bare legs, down to my knees, up between my thighs, forcing my legs apart a little more. He cups my ass with his hands, his thumbs swirling over my hips.

Hades licks his lips, and I swear his mouth is watering for a taste. But while he stares at my pussy as if he were a starving man and I was a feast, he places a gentle kiss on my inner thigh, featherlight, a whisper of a touch that makes my knees go weak.

Before I can fall, vines shoot up from the ground, wrapping up my shins, curling behind my thighs, cradling my backside as I stumble. I'm now reclining on a bed of leaves and vines that I apparently summoned, my legs spread wide open right in front of Hades's mouth.

He glances up at me, his eyebrow cocked wickedly.

And then his hands glide over me, parting my folds, exposing me fully to him, and he lowers his head to my pussy, sliding a long, luxurious lick up my cunt, lingering on my clit. He swirls his tongue over my clit, sucking softly, humming, and I'm already gasping for air, unable to fully comprehend what's happening.

The plants, however, seem to know *exactly* how to help. Vines curl over my thighs, pushing my legs wider, my knees higher, serving my cunt up to Hades. He chuckles, and the vibrations shoot right up my clit. I suck in air, already nearly screaming with pleasure, and then Hades plunges his fingers into me, curling them inside my body in a way that makes his tongue on my clit even *more* than before. The vines cup my body, tightening so I cannot squirm away, and a part of me is aware that the plants are making this orgasm even better, and another part of me is aware that *I* am the one controlling the vines, controlling the way my body, even now, *must* accept the pleasure Hades is stroking inside my body, licking over my clit, and the idea that this is happening—*all* of this—makes me keen with pleasure, my back arching up.

The vines keep my legs spread wide open, giving Hades the exact right access to my body. His fingers stroke inside me, his tongue laves over that tightly coiled bundle of nerves, and my whole body is vibrating with pleasure, a rhythm that the plants take on. I open my eyes as the soft red petals of the roses shake free, falling over my tightly wound body.

And Hades *hums* his pleasure into me, and everything *shatters*. I scream his name, the orgasm making my entire body quake. The roses burst, every remaining petal cascading over us.

"I have her," Hades says, and the vines that had been holding me open for him pull away, pushing my body gently into his embrace. My skin is still too sensitive; his very touch makes me gasp. But he wraps his strong arms around me and holds me until I can stop shaking, until even the rose petals are still.

CHAPTER 8
HADES

In the fading quivers of Josie's orgasm, the thorned branches retract into the ground. The roses spiral in on themselves. The vines, greenery, all the beauty she made—it pulls away like curtains parting, and we are left, her and I, on the bank of the river, her soft body pliant in my arms.

I hold her tight until her relaxed muscles begin to tense again, coming back to awareness. But even then, I do not let go, my own muscles rigid in shock that I cannot break through, not yet.

Nothing happens quickly down here. We are not immortal, but we live long enough that time is meaningless, and so we do not rush or fall into things abruptly because why would we?

So this, too, is new, new in a crash and a shatter and a destructive eruption.

I can still taste her on my tongue, her sugared sweetness. I can still feel the shudders of her body as she came apart in my mouth.

And I know, with that taste and those shudders resonating in me, that I will be chasing those sensations from her for the rest of my almost endless existence.

She has been in the Underworld, in my arms, for a few hours only.

And I am wholly hers already.

"Hades?" Josie touches my cheek. I have been staring at the bank of the river, the grass uncovered now from her vines, her robes back in place over her body.

The difference between the magically-generated plant life we have here and Josie's true springing greenery is startling. I'd always known our trees and plants were dull and gray, existing from descriptions passed down by those who long ago knew what the surface looked like. But to see the shock of vibrancy, and now to have it retract—

Protectiveness surges through me. She will be desired here for what she can do. There are those who would immediately abuse or manipulate her, like Zoticus; and even beyond them, there are many who are harmless but would do anything to see such life again.

She will be in danger.

But she is under my protection. And so she will be *safe*.

I stand, lifting her to her feet, and when I set her down, I straighten her gown, movements stiff.

I had Agapi call the council.

Like a gods-damned fool.

The council's opinion does not matter. Josie is under my protection. I do not need to hear their useless prattling about what should be done about her or her mother—

That does, briefly, sober me.

Demeter is on Earth, wandering free. Though she has caused no trouble for mortals, she caused pain to *Josie*, in not telling her what she truly is, and that —*that* I cannot allow to go unaddressed.

"My council will be gathered now," I tell her, my eyes meeting hers. There is worry in her now, a slight frown of concern.

I put my thumb on the edge of her lips.

"Trust me, Josie," I say to her. "They will only wish to hear your story. It is unusual for a demigod to walk freely on Earth. And your mother—"

"What about my mother?" Josie's eyebrows bend slightly.

I brush my fingers across that crease. "She is a goddess. She, too, belongs here."

"Belongs—in the Underworld?" Josie shakes her head. "Wait—*too*? I belong here?"

Yes. Yes, with me. Can't you feel it? You must feel it, too.

"Come," I say instead. "I must address a few things with my council. Then I will explain our purpose here."

I will have to keep her in this cage. Her, this brilliant burst of life and greenery, golden hair and hypnotic eyes. I will have to imprison her. And her mother.

"Come," I say again, and I take her hand.

Agapi has indeed gathered my council. The representative chosen of every god line—save for Zeus, now, as Zoticus is rightfully rotting in my dungeon. Almost a dozen demigods stand in my throne room as I walk Josie up the long marble floor, magically induced light glowing through windows in lieu of the sun.

I rise up the dais, and without hesitating, pull Josie into my lap as I sit.

She gasps, a small, winded inhalation, but she does not argue, does not push away.

My fingers curl into the supple skin of her thigh.

"A daughter of Demeter has found her way to us," I tell my council. And I explain what they likely already know—that Zoticus abducted her, that she came from Earth, that this means Demeter is indeed still walking freely above our domain.

There is a long pause after I explain Josie's power display on the riverbank. I do not tell them about how I calmed her down—that is not theirs to know or imagine, and I find myself growing childishly angry at the idea that anyone else might try or even envision something similar with her. She is mine to protect here, mine to help.

She adjusts on my lap, and I feel the hardness of my cock driving against her ass, made even harder by the way she flicks her eyes to the side, to me, and rolls her lower lip between her teeth.

I clamp my fingers to her thigh, rubbing a circle through the gauzy fabric.

"What will be done?" one of my councilors asks. A descendant of Artemis.

Josie looks at me fully, her eyes wide and hopeful and still afraid. I watch her, mind spiraling, spiraling, through everything I must do, through everything I *want* to do, and those things clash up against one another.

I must keep her here.

I must drag her mother here as well.

I want to make her fall apart, again, again, to soothe away the concern and worry creasing her face. She should only ever know pleasure, bliss.

For a moment, I envy the gods trapped across the Lethe. But that envy breaks apart through me—to live in only endless bliss is no life at all.

Pain is a part of existence.

Is what we have down here existence, though? It is a half-life. Part of one and shades of another.

And though Josie does seem angry at her mother for lying to her, what will she feel when Demeter is dragged here and thrown across the Lethe and reduced to a blubbering shell of need and ignorance? That is the fate of all the full gods, the only way to ensure humanity is safe on Earth. And Josie will stay here, on this side of Lethe, a demigod in a kinder cage, but still a cage.

Before any move is made, Josie deserves to understand fully what is happening to her. I will not be another being to disappoint her.

I will earn her trust, and I will not break it.

I stand from the throne, depositing Josie on the floor beside me. "Plans will be delayed for now. I have much to discuss with our new guest."

Guest. As though she would be able to leave.

Questions arise from my council. At the edge of the room, Agapi watches, their eyes dark in confusion and concern.

I ignore everyone and pull Josie through the palace, the twisting halls that go from marble to onyx to brilliant gold, ever changing on the whims of past rulers who altered wings for their tastes. I haven't made any such mark on this place.

We reach an exterior door and emerge back outside, though closer to the opposite river. The Lethe.

Josie has been silent as I guided her through the palace. Now, though, she comes up alongside me, matching my quickened pace. "Hades? What do you need to talk about with me?"

I walk. Keep walking. We weave through out buildings around the palace, then a few winding streets take us to that road I followed yesterday, down through the forest, to the bank of the Lethe.

There is a new guard now, thanks to Orfeas.

I stop, panting, though not from the fast walk. From the way Josie is watching me, her face hardening more, as if I have told her what her fate is now, and how it is my duty to enact it.

The new guard sees me and nods, stepping farther away, giving me space without prompt.

I point across the riverbank, to the distance but visible peaks of buildings. "Tartarus."

Josie follows my direction. She sees it, looks back at me, unaffected. "All right?"

"Hades—the original—imprisoned his god siblings centuries ago," I explain, my voice deadened. My pointing arm falls heavily to my side. I want to take her hand again. She will hate me after I say this. "It is the law he enacted, the price demanded for the sacrifice of protecting Earth from the vengeful, aggressive cruelty of the gods. That every god be locked in blissful ignorance fed by the Lethe's waters, and everyone of god blood be confined to the Underworld."

I turn to her, seeing if she understands.

Josie's brow is bent again, that crease signaling rising confusion, or maybe displeasure.

"Your mother is one of the few gods who escaped his final machinations to ensnare his siblings," I say. "It is one of my tasks, has been the task of every ancestor of mine, to find and bring her here."

Realization dawns on her face. *Dawns* is an unfair word—nothing about her features brightens. She is all darkness and dread.

"You are going to capture my mother and bring her—there?" She looks across again, at the distant village.

"Yes."

"What would happen to her?"

What *would* happen, not what *will* happen.

I swallow. "She will forget who she is. What she wants, all but the basest desires and affects. She will be reduced to a harmless shell."

Josie's darkness turns pointed. At me. "My mother has done nothing wrong. She doesn't harm anyone, least of all—least of all *mortals*. She's not always the best person, and she lied to me, but she doesn't deserve *this*."

"I am bound by the duties of my ancestors," I say. "I am bound by—"

"To hell with your duties! What the fuck does that even mean? It's been *centuries* since your ancestor created this prison, and my mother has done nothing wrong." A pause. The barest hesitation. "Has she? You'd have heard, wouldn't you? If she was up there raping and pillaging like the other gods used to?"

The muscles in my neck are so tense they ache. "Yes. I would have heard."

"And did you?"

"No."

Josie waves her arms as if to say *Well, there you have it, then*. "So why do you need to disturb her at all? She's proven she's fine to be left on Earth."

Her posture relaxes, safe in her argument, but I do not back down. Cannot.

"Keeping the gods here is the task the first Hades left to his demigod descendants," I say, words echoing in my ears, as though my father is speaking them through me. Disgust roils in my gut. "It is my charge. No other Hades has failed in it."

"And this would be a failure? How? It's not like she escaped."

"She is meant to be here. For the protection of mortals."

Josie's anger starts to return, seeing that I won't concede her point.

She faces me fully. "Are you, like, magically compelled to do this? Though I doubt that, considering you haven't been forced to find her before now."

"It's more complicated than that. Josie, I don't—"

"So it's a choice. You're *choosing* to go after her, even though she's been *fine* for centuries. How is that any sort of justice?"

"It isn't meant to be justice. It's meant to give mortals the best chance possible. And that chance only comes if all gods are locked away."

"But my mother *hasn't been hurting anyone.*"

"That is not a risk I can take. If other demigods heard that I allowed Demeter to continue living on land, anarchy would ensue. If she is trusted to be free, why not others? It is a disastrous slope, Josie. She must be brought here."

She draws back, scowling, eyes shifting through mine. "No. No, that's not it. This is a power trip. Do you get off on this?"

My turn to darken. She notes the change in my

expression, honing in on it with precision, and I would be impressed if not for the welling revulsion that tinges in the back of my throat. I know what she will say, the guess she will make, but even so, it disgusts me.

"You like keeping the gods imprisoned and weak so you can fuck around in pretend elitism. That one that abducted me—that's the norm here, isn't it? You're just as bad. Just as bad as—"

I lurch towards her, barely restraining myself from grabbing her, but my movement silences her.

But I turn, fuming, and get a two paces away before I glare back at her. "Follow me."

She seethes. Few people dare to challenge me. Few of those last so long in argument with me, but Josie's fury doesn't dim, and I can't deny the infusing effect it has on my desire for her. She doesn't cower, doesn't back down.

"Follow me," I repeat, harder. "That was not a question."

"A command?" she sneers. "I'm not one of your demigods."

"Yes, you are."

I turn again, walking, knowing she will follow.

She is not the first of us to believe that the world would not suffer if the gods were released, if we did away with our bindings that keep us here. If we unleashed ourselves back on the world. That argument has been used before, by demigods desperate to be on Earth.

Do they think I enjoy it here? Do they think I do not *want* to see the sun again?

Those who claim that things were not as bad as we make them out to be have forgotten just how abysmal the gods can be. They have short memories, drowned in ambrosia and wine.

I envy them.

I envy those who were sired by demigods who had less of their original god's blood. I envy those who have grown up here with any kind of *hope* that gods are not as depraved as we have been told.

When anyone brings that argument to my feet, I tell them to spend time in Asphodel Meadows. I *order* them to go there, to see the aftermath they have either forgotten or never experienced, and usually that is enough to silence their complaints. Zoticus alone visited Asphodel Meadows and returned unaffected.

So I know, as I hear the soft footsteps of Josie following me, that showing her this will not only silence her argument, but will wake her up to the reality of what she is. Of what I am.

Not merely demigods.

But monsters.

CHAPTER 9
JOSIE

know what Asphodel Meadows is, of course. Despite the Underworld being different from my studies, there are enough parallels for me to figure out at least the general intent of things.

In Ancient Greek mythology, the afterlife was split up much differently from how most American Christians see death. There was no heaven or hell, no one place of good and one place of bad. Instead, in Ancient Greek, the Underworld—which was called that because it was literally under the world, as this cave system appears to be—was a sort of ranked hierarchy. The rivers connected everything. Heroes and people worthy of being ranked above others got to go to Elysium Fields, where drinking from the Mnemosyne meant they relived their glory days in perpetuity. Tartarus contained the worst souls and the worst monsters, a place where the gods could keep an eye out on their enemies.

But Asphodel Meadows was a sort of middle ground. If you were average, which to be fair, most of us are, death was supposed to be a gentle retirement in the gray, shady area of Asphodel Meadows, named for the white blooms of the asphodel flower.

I'm quiet as I walk beside Hades, thinking of everything he's said, but also everything I saw when I drank from the River Mnemosyne.

I understand that when the gods walked on Earth, it was dangerous. There's irony in the fact that my research project was supposed to prove that the gods were fake, and if any average Ancient Greek had bothered to walk up a mountain, they could have proven it for themselves—knowing just how wrong I was in that assumption really makes me recast my vision for my doctorate. If only Dr. Phillips could see me now . . .

I draw up short as Hades pauses.

Asphodel Meadows is crowded, but no one seems to mind. Each person—or shade of a person, because no one here is still alive—has their own space and is seemingly oblivious to the others, as if each were in their own bubble of reality. Some talk to the air, some muse in silence, some have pale, blank eyes that rove around, seeing something no one else can see.

It's eerie. I rub my arms, chilled to my core despite the warm air.

"Asphodel Meadows was considered a mercy by the original Hades," this Hades, my Hades, says, his eyes watching the different shades.

"It's so . . . unnatural," I manage.

"It lets them forget," Hades says, as if that were answer enough.

"What do you mean, forget?" I ask.

Hades reaches his hand out, pulling, and for a moment, I get a sense of his power. I see before me a big field with hundreds of people in it, yes, but the Underworld is like the Tardis from *Doctor Who:* bigger on the inside. The scope is infinite, more than my mortal mind can understand.

My mind is not only mortal, I think, and the demigod part of me that has lain dormant for so long awakens, heightening my understanding.

"Not every mortal who ever dies comes here," Hades tells me as the field shifts and blends, expanding and narrowing. "Only the ones who choose this as their afterlife."

"Who would choose this?" I mutter, but Hades hears me.

The spinning stops, and I look down at the shade sitting nearest us. She wears classical clothing, and has a handloom in her lap.

"Arachne," Hades says. The shade doesn't seem to show us that she hears. "Athena was jealous of her weaving and turned her into a spider for centuries. Once Athena was captured and . . . contained, I was able to save Arachne and bring her here, letting her forget the torture."

I frown as I watch Arachne, humming to herself. Arachne was renowned for her weaving skills, turned into a legend that survived all the way to my time. But the cloth in her lap now is plain white, dull and nothing special. That doesn't seem like the type of weaving a goddess would be jealous of.

"Europa," Hades continued, gesturing to another woman, then another and another. "Callisto. Antiope."

"I know what they have in common," I whisper. Each of the shades is in their own spot of the meadow, each one quietly swaying or humming or braiding flowers into crowns, all idle and mindless. Each one of them had been a victim of Zeus's lust, their victimhood becoming a cautionary tale against how willing Zeus was to rape whomever he decided he wanted.

"It wasn't just Zeus," Hades says. He points to another woman. "Theophane." Raped by Poseidon. Hades points to another. "Erigone." A victim of Dionysus. "More." He waves his hand out at the field full of mostly women, but some men. All of them victims of the gods' whims.

"But Zeus is contained now," I say. "They all are. Right?"

"Yes." Hades says it firmly, looking down at me. "You're safe, Josie."

"But so are these women, right?" I press. "Why are they trapped in this half-life?"

"It's a path of their own choosing," he says. His voice drops, even though there's no one around us but the shades of the dead, and they seem oblivious to our presence. "It's a mercy to them, to forget."

I cock my head. "Maybe at first," I say. "But . . . now? After so many centuries? Antiope had a life after Zeus raped her, a family. Arachne was an artist. These women exist outside of the trauma of their pasts, and wiping their memories of the bad has also destroyed all their hopes of reliving the good."

"Josie, you don't understand—" Hades starts, but I shake my head.

"No, *you* don't understand. It's bad enough that these people get defined by their victimhood, but wiping their memories is not the solution."

"It's Asphodel Meadows, Josie," Hades says gently. He's treating me like an ignorant child, and it's making my blood boil. "The point is that these people want to forget."

All right, so Psych 101 isn't a course offered to the Greek Underworld. "Look, I get what you're saying," I grind out, frustrated, "but you have to see this isn't sustainable, right? Yes, the gods are bad. I agree! Zeus is like, king of all dicks of all time. They *obviously* did bad things—but this is also bad, Hades." I search his eyes, begging for him to understand. "If these shades were given a chance to keep their memories, they'd also retain the memories of what they loved. Art and music and friends and family. You can't take away one without the other."

There's something calculating in Hades's eyes, something I don't like. "I took you here, Josie, to show you why the gods need to be locked away. And you agree, yes, that they do need to be contained."

"I do, but—"

"So you understand, then, why I am going to have to bring your mother to the Underworld and trap her." He takes a deep, shaky breath. "And you understand also why you're going to have to stay here."

"A prisoner?"

A pained expression flashes in his eyes. "The side of the rivers we—the demigods, the children of the gods—live on does not involve the same chains the full gods must wear. But even a drop of god blood means you are a risk to the Earth above."

I had understood, on some level, what Hades had meant before. But this—no. *No.* I have a life on Earth, a good one, a life I love. And Mom . . . she may be overbearing, but she does *good* on Earth. Hades has no idea the good she's done, feeding the homeless, helping at the women's shelter, selflessly aiding the community. She's not cruel like the gods of old, even if she was one of them.

Neither of us deserve to be prisoners.

CHAPTER 10
HADES

The next evening, Agapi plans a feast for Josie.

I should have thought of such a thing, but my mind is in tatters, ripped by her mere presence here first, then shredded further by her argument in Asphodel Meadows.

"Yes, the gods are bad. They obviously did bad things —but this is also bad, Hades."

Her words ring in my head as I numbly dress for the banquet.

This is also bad, Hades.

She'd glared at me with accusation, with contempt, with the kind of disgust I know I deserve. She *saw* me, all the vile blood of my ancestry—but still, she believes that what I am doing in keeping everyone of god blood trapped here is wrong.

I arrange the black silk of my toga in a jerky tug, scowling at my reflection. Agapi laid out the clothing. Traditional nonsense no one wears anymore—so likely the whole feast will be a throwback to the days of old, our history we only know from scrolls and tales. But I look at my dark eyes in the mirror, dressed as I am, and I imagine my ancestors, all of them, each one pressing more and more weight onto my shoulders.

This is our task. Our only task. The Hades line keeps the world safe. We are trapped here, but it is a small punishment compared to the hell gods wrought on mortals.

So whatever suffering I feel over Josie's earned anger is minimal. I will accept it.

It is no less than I deserve.

But what does she deserve? And what does Agapi deserve, and Orfeas, and all the other demigods here?

Lost in thought, I find myself back in the throne room with no memory of having gotten there.

The room has been transformed, the heavy darkness of the onyx and black aura cut through with airy white gauze and gleaming torches, lush lounging pillows and low tables spread with the finest food, scenting the air with sweetness and salt. Other demigods are trickling in already, our arrival accompanied by the hum of musicians on lyres and harps.

I stop next to where Agapi is talking with a server about the arrangement of beverages on a platter.

"You have outdone yourself," I tell them.

They twist a gleaming grin at me, their hair done up in tight curls, lips bright red to match the scarlet tunic braided around their body. "It isn't often I get to put my skills to use like this."

"We have parties constantly."

They give me a flat stare. "For something *worthwhile*, I mean. For someone *new*."

For a new prisoner, I want to say, but it is nice to see them smiling. I hadn't realized how long it had been since I'd seen Agapi smile like this, truly, but the oddity of their grin catches me into silence.

I cast my eyes around the room again. More than a dozen demigods are gathered, seated at the table already, indulging in the drink and food, the party underway without any official start. We have enough parties, just as Agapi said, that formality is few and far between, and even if the cause for this one is different—*new*—it still leaves a foul taste in my mouth.

"Are you happy here?" I ask Agapi.

Orfeas comes up behind them and threads his

arms around Agapi's waist in time to hear my question.

Agapi flinches, so quickly I almost miss it. But they give a smile, one that is more performative. "As much as any living creature is happy where they are planted, I suppose."

"But there are things you desire elsewhere. If you could. On Earth."

They lean back into Orfeas, who is watching me, brow furrowed.

"Well, yes," Agapi says slowly. They bat their hand dismissively. "But we have all we need here."

Needs met, yes.

But why can't we long for more?

Orfeas whispers something into Agapi's ear that makes them blush, lips parting to respond—

They stop.

Agapi and Orfeas both clock something across the room, then their eyes simultaneously flick to me.

Agapi's grin goes sly.

So I know before I turn that she is here.

Josie was given a whole suite in the palace. The finest lodgings, as though that will make her imprisonment here any softer. I know it will do nothing to change her mind on what is happening, and I wonder if she even is offended that I tried to buy her off with gorgeous rooms. I was too much a coward to stay and see her reaction; I had servants take her to the rooms when we returned last night.

So I have not seen her since Asphodel Meadows. Have not spoken to her since our argument surrounded by the static souls of the gods' worst victims.

Josie enters through a side door. Her chin is high, eyes snapping in alert analysis over the room, and it is her poise that seizes me first. Her hair is in perfect ringlets, the kind I can too easily imagine twisting around my fingers, her face glistening with gold dust on her cheekbones and eyelids, her lips ruby red, like Agapi's. Her gown is gold, a tunic of silk that hangs from one shoulder, the fabric lighter and more form fitting than silk—it clings to her curves like liquid, so decadent I can see the dip of her navel, the indentation in each hip.

Her eyes find mine. And we both just stare at one another, locked in a sort of fog where I cannot read the expression on her face.

"Go to her, you idiot," Agapi hisses.

"I don't think he's breathing, love," Orfeas whispers, a bit loudly.

"Is this what a smitten Hades looks like?"

"Embarrassing, I daresay."

"Look, his cheeks are pink—"

"Shut up, you both," I snap.

The bite of my voice cuts through the levity they tried to create. Orfeas unwinds himself from Agapi and frowns at me, his features sharpening in a soldier's quick calculation.

"You fucked something up," he guesses. "Fix it."

I have an idea of how to fix it, with Josie.

But doing so may just break everything my ancestors worked for, everything I am duty bound to uphold.

The alternative, though, is for her to hate me into eternity, and that even one night spent testing those waters was unbearable.

I nod at Orfeas and manage a halfhearted smile of agreement. It makes Orfeas's brow raise, and I wonder when last they saw me smile, too.

I cross the room to where Josie is still by the door, unmoved.

At my approach, she folds her arms across her chest. "Hades," she says when I stop in front of her. Then she gives a mockery of a bow. "Or should I say *my lord*? How should I address my captor? I've never been someone's prisoner before."

My chest clenches. "You are not my prisoner."

Josie's eyes narrow. "You hold the keys. You aren't letting me leave."

We are off to the side of the room, the banquet in

earnest behind us, demigods in the full swing of a party. Music plays still, light and uplifting, and it alleviates some of the strain in my heart.

"You saw Asphodel Meadows." I don't know why I'm still trying. These words sound weak even to my own ears. "You know what the gods are capable of, and why they must be restrained."

"But I'm not like that," Josie counters. "And . . . I don't think you are, either."

It catches me so off guard that I go silent, lips parted. "You know nothing about me."

She blushes. A beautiful flare of scarlet. "That's hardly true." She sniffs before I can indulge that train of thought, the pulse of desire that goes straight to my cock. "I mean—in the time I've been here, you don't strike me as someone who's being restrained from rampaging over mortals."

"No, of course—"

"Then why are you keeping yourself here? You can't just imprison people because of their blood."

"You said you are a student of our myths," I say, jaw tight. "Knowing our history, how can you say such a thing? The same evil that propelled the gods to fill Asphodel Meadows is inside of me."

"That's bullshit." Josie angles closer to me, rage sparking in her eyes. "That's bullshit, and you know it. Evil is a choice, not a genetic flaw, and you're letting the mistakes of a few dictate the lives of the many. What kind of ruler does that?"

I go silent. Watching her anger, the hypnotic light in her eyes, and I find all of my usual arguments withering, as they have been since she arrived, since I started noticing Agapi's unhappiness, Orfeas's longing, all the little bits and pieces slowly building up to tell me that this existence is incomplete. That the way I have been ruling here, the duty I swore to, is insufficient.

"I have been shortsighted," I hear myself say.

Josie draws back in surprise. Did she not expect me to agree? I certainly didn't.

I turn away, hand on my chin as I survey the banquet room again. The demigods are laughing. Smiling. They are not *unhappy* here, as Agapi noted—we have everything we need.

But we could have more.

And I have never truly let myself believe that until this moment.

"You and your mother have proven trustworthy on Earth," I say to Josie, a plan forming. "But I cannot simply allow you to go, not without upsetting the balance of the Underworld. I propose something of a trial situation instead."

When I turn my gaze back to her, she is watching me curiously, her anger fully gone in favor of cautious observation.

"You can return to Earth for, say, half a year, after which you will return to update me on you and your mother's existence on Earth for the remainder of the year. This way, I can keep tabs on you, so it does not look as though I am doing you any special favors."

And, if this works out with her, then I can begin toying with the idea of rippling it out to others as well.

"Half a year?" Josie frowns. "I'd still be a prisoner for six months?"

"An ambassador, more like. A connection between demigods here, in the Underworld, and your mother on Earth. A way to test some of us reentering the mortal realm. It must be done slowly—you have proven yourself worthy of being on Earth, but other demigods? They will need to see that if we are to do this, it will be monitored and any errant behavior immediately punished."

Her eyebrows go up. Not in shock or disgust, but in consideration.

I keep on, lungs tensing with this building plan, the hope I can feel blooming to life in my gut. *Hope.* How long since I felt hope? Possibly never.

"Because you are right," I say. "You are right that

we do not deserve to be punished for the sins of our ancestors. And this, I think, could be the way out."

A small smile tugs at the edge of Josie's lips. "When would I be allowed back on Earth?"

My jaw works. "You would need to make yourself known to my council for a time, to get them on board with this idea. If you are willing to do this, to become my ambassador, then you will need to ingratiate yourself into our society here, to understand fully what it is you are taking on—"

"Is there another option?" Her face flickers. "I accept this role or—what?"

My teeth clench. If she refuses, if she demands that she have her whole freedom or nothing, then what?

"If this is unsatisfactory to you," I start, "then we can discuss other arrangements. But I—I had hoped you would see the gravity in this situation. I had hoped you would see that your presence here, and on Earth, is not as simple as you once believed. I'm sorry. I wish I could change that."

Josie is silent for a long moment, her eyes shifting through mine, weighing my words. I brace for argument.

But her eyes go, briefly, beyond my shoulder, to the demigods laughing boisterously at the tables.

Her eyes go back to mine. "Six months. Starting

now?"

"If it pleases you."

"None of this is *pleasing*." But she shrugs. "And you'll leave my mother alone during this?"

As a demigod, per the ancient laws, Josie would be on this side of the River Lethe, feasting and living a more or less free life. But her mother, as an original god, would be forced to drink Lethe's waters, forget her past, forget her daughter, and be truly a prisoner with no will.

"As long as she continues in her peaceful existence, yes," I promise. "That will be part of the trial we propose to my council."

"Can I talk to her? To let her know about what's happening."

I nod. "I can arrange that."

"All right." She nods. "I agree."

The breath kicks out of my chest. "You will?"

She smiles. It's a brief flash of amusement, and it stirs my cock to life again, that sight of white teeth against red, red lips. "You expected me to argue?"

"Yes."

Josie laughs. She laughs, and it is utterly unfair that such a simple noise is capable of destroying me so efficiently.

"Honestly?" Josie smiles again. "It's not actually that big of a sacrifice for me to make. On Earth, I researched Greek mythology, so to actually be *here*—it's better than any archaeological dig."

"You researched us?" I echo her smile.

Something about my question, or maybe my reaction, has Josie staring at my face for a beat longer than I expect.

Her hand grips onto mine and she edges a bit closer to my body.

I want to have this conversation with her. I want to hear everything she has to say.

But I am also vividly, painfully aware of my hardening cock in this loose tunic, of the closeness of Josie's hot body, of the way she licks her pink tongue on her full bottom lip.

"Yes," she says. "I researched you. Well, not *you.* The gods."

"I am a sad replacement for your studies, then."

Her smile slips away and she shakes her head. "Hardly."

My body shakes, fingers aching, and I think I will fall to pieces if I don't touch her.

I extend my hand. I don't even know what I am asking of her, where I would take her, but I wait, palm out.

Josie looks at that hand. She sips in a breath.

When she lays her palm against mine, the heat of her skin temporarily numbs me.

"Josie," I say her name, I have to, and it grates against the winding tension in my throat.

Her wide eyes fix on me, the increasing cadence of her gasps showing in the rise and fall of her chest beneath that skin-tight gown.

"What will I do," she starts, a throaty whisper, "while I am here? Meet with your council, I imagine. What else?"

"I'll help you learn what you need to know about us."

"I already know quite a lot about you."

Ah, that is true.

I smile. It is slow and languid as my fingers close around her, thumb stroking against the velvet skin across the back of her hand. "Whatever you like, then." A pause. "What would you like to see of the Underworld? Anything. I lay it all at your feet."

Josie gasps a little. "At my feet?" Her eyes take on a twist of coyness so visceral I feel it in the tip of my groin.

I lift my other hand and glide just the edge of my thumb along her jaw. "Need I prove it to you again? I will, Josie."

Her gaze snaps away, dipping quickly around the

room, and before she can ask the question I see forming in her eyes, I run my thumb down the center of her neck.

"If you think anyone here has qualms with public sex, you grossly miscalculate the sheer boredom that comes with decades of sameness. But if you prefer privacy, we can easily—"

"You do this sort of thing a lot, do you?" The question is hung with a dozen others.

I step closer, closer, until my body is flush with hers, and I know she can feel the hardness of my prick rubbing against the apex of her thighs, because I can feel the heat of her there, the alluring warmth of her cunt already aching for me.

"I do not do this sort of thing a lot," I tell her. "Orgies, on occasion. But with you? Josie." I bend down, wanting to pour out how much she has changed things for me, not sure how to formulate something so expansive. "I have been waiting for you for some time, I think," I finally say, my voice breaking in earnestness.

Her hand comes up and threads around my wrist where I have her slender neck in my grasp. The way she meets my eyes is a lurch, a demand, and my mouth goes dry.

"This banquet is in my honor, right? Someone— Agapi? They said that's why we're here."

"Mm."

"Then this is for me," she repeats. Her grip on my wrist tightens, pressing my hand more firmly around her throat. "So lay yourself at my feet, Hades. Make my time in the Underworld worthwhile."

CHAPTER 11
JOSIE

Hades replaces his hand at my throat with his lips. I tilt back, giving him better access, but even as I want to get lost in this moment, I force my eyes to focus around the room.

There are dozens of people here—no, not people. Demigods. *Like me.* The thought comes unbidden, and a flare of panic shoots through me, replacing everything else. Tiny white flowers cascade around Hades and me, a rain of scented petals.

It draws every single eye to us.

"We are not used to new beauty in the Underworld," Hades murmurs.

My gaze flicks over the room. I've never really been an exhibitionist, but . . . the idea that everyone is watching me, *us* . . . the coil of anticipation and longing winds tighter inside of me. Hades had told me that we could have privacy, but . . .

I don't want it.

Hades flicks the shell of my ear with his tongue, the sensation drawing a soft moan from my lips and a flurry of petals from my fingers. Some members of the crowd watching us gasp or applaud at this little show of my powers.

My powers.

I'm a demigod, and I am seeing just how appealing it is to be worshiped.

Hades nips at my neck, his tongue sliding over my throat. "How far do you wish to take this?" he asks gently.

"All the way."

He pauses, checking to make sure I mean my answer. "I do not mind the others watching," he says, his voice low and only for me, "but I do not want to share."

"Same," I answer pertly. The corner of his lips twist up, his grin eager.

He dips his head to my clavicle, enticing me with gentle kisses as his rough fingers tug at my tunic, releasing the brooch that held it at my shoulders. The white cloth falls away easily, exposing my body, flushed with desire, to everyone in the feast hall. Before I have a chance to register the cool air on my skin, Hades' lips have found my left nipple, his hand cupping my right breast. I arch back, relishing the sensation.

Dimly, I see others in the crowd turning to their own partners, playing with each other as Hades plays with me.

I fight a little frown. I don't mind the way their bodies seek release, but I want their attention. Let them fuck as they want; I want their eyes on me.

How far things have changed, I think, a moment of clarity breaking into my thoughts as I gaze out at the demigods watching Hades and me. I have spent so much of my life aware of my mother's constant gaze and her overprotective nature, and now, when I find myself forcibly separated from her in this other realm, where I know I will have half a year to discover myself . . .

No. I won't overthink it. It is enough for me to be here, now, in this moment.

With this man.

And the eyes of the Underworld on me.

It is enough for me to discover my powers as a demigod. To relish in them.

To be worshiped for them.

We are in a stone hall, but my magic does not require earth for plants to grow. Life falls from my power; plants take root in unbroken marble, moss creating a soft coolness at our feet, vines winding up over us. Hades breaks from me in surprise, his eyes widening. I see respect in his gaze. For me. For my power.

Oh, a girl could get used to that.

"What do you have in mind?" Hades asks me in a low voice.

I am discovering new things about myself all the time. And right now, it's all about power.

"I'll take the lead," I say.

His arms tighten around me, and I feel his hard cock through the thin cloth of our robes. Hades is always in control; I think having me take over is as enticing to him as it is for me. "We need a word, though," he says, his breath hot on my ear.

Of course, I know the legends of my Hades's predecessor. I know what it means when I whisper back to him, "Pomegranate."

His lips curve up. "I say that, or you say that, and the game is over," he says, establishing our safe word.

I nod, agreeing. As I do so, the vines curl up, wrapping around Hades's ankles. I feel the plants as an extension of me, and where the green touches his skin, I feel it, too, a magical connection between us.

I nudge Hades's ankles with my feet, and the vines spread his legs apart for me. More vines shoot up, these wrapping around his wrists as he starts to reach for me. "Right now," I tell him when his eyes open in surprise, "you're mine, and I shall do exactly as I like."

He groans in agreement, and I hear the gasps and moans of our audience. I know I have their attention as I carefully pull the metal pin that holds Hades's robes on his shoulders, letting the cloth drop off his body and pool at his feet.

He is a demigod, but the way his body looks now is unholy. Hades is made of hard muscle, the veins of his arm popping up as he shifts and my vines hold him steady. I run my hand over his tanned skin, feeling him. His cock twitches in response, huge and dripping and *begging.*

It's excruciating for me to move so slowly over him. My pussy clenches; I *want* him, I need him, but I am too busy loving this anticipation. Let the coil wind tighter. It will make the release all the better.

There's not a sound from the audience I trace over his chest, my fingers bumping over the distinct, firm lines of his six-pack, trailing through the thin hair that leads down to his groin. I swirl my touch past his hard cock, over his tense thighs. I'm positively dripping with desire for him, but as I lower to my knees in front of him, I can tell that our audience is even more eager. I hear a woman's gasp of pleasure, a deep-throated groan from a man as they please themselves and each other, watching as I lower my head to eye-level with Hades's dripping cock.

Soft-petalled flowers and mounds of springy moss and cushioning leaves burst at my knees, giving me a floral pillow as I position myself at Hades's feet. I feel perfectly at ease, eager even, as I flick out my tongue and lick his shaft from root to tip, swirling over the hot liquid dripping from his cock. Hades groans, long and loud, and the vines twist around his legs and arms, pulling him closer to me.

I part my lips and take his full length in my mouth.

Vines shoot up around Hades's hips, pulling and tugging him so that I don't have to strain. I relax my throat, feeling him filling me, and I hum with pleasure. The vibrations to his cock make him groan louder, and when I make the vines tighten even more, digging into his skin just a little, just enough to be felt, I can feel his knees start to buckle. My plants support him, keeping his body perfectly positioned for both our pleasure.

I lean back, sucking hard. With a slight *pop* of my lips as I pull out, I watch Hades shudder, the cold air replacing my warm mouth. Before he can fully take in the sensation, I plunge down, licking his cock as it slides into my mouth. He's so *big*, and my eyes water with the strain of taking him.

With my mouth full of his cock, I raise my eyes to Hades. His whole body is straining toward me, but held in place by my plants. He meets my eyes, and I see nothing but pure and true adoration for me, for what I can do for him.

"Please," he begs.

In reward, I work my mouth, pressing my tongue against his shaft as I move up and down over his cock.

"*Please!*" The cry rips out of him, begging, and behind me, I become aware of the audience again. The moans of pleasure from the demigods watching us are interspersed now with the wet, heavy sounds of fucking. The entire hall drips with lust, with unmet need.

I pull back long enough to look around me, the taste of his cum on my lips.

No one in the entire room has had release.

Not yet.

Not until *I* let them have it.

This is a power the likes of which I have never felt before.

And I cannot get enough.

CHAPTER 12
HADES

If there had been any doubt as to Josie's lineage, I would need only look down at her to know she is a goddess.

Her swollen pink lips. Her cheeks flushed scarlet as they hollow and extend around my cock. Her glistening, intent eyes fixed up on me, and that connection alone is enough to push me dangerously close to release.

But I refrain, muscles contracting, as Josie gives my cock one last lick, her eyes rolling back in her head in her own pleasure. I moan, held fully in her vines.

Of the orgies I have participated in, I usually play a more dominant role. It is expected of me, of my position, and so I never questioned it—but now, with Josie so very clearly in charge, her eyes lighting with erotic mischief, I am shoved into a new kind of absence of self, body feeling untethered, buoyant. The mantle of responsibility is not one I ever thought could be removed—but it is, *she* has removed it, if only for this moment, and I fall willingly, eagerly.

Josie runs her hands up my chest, tweaking a nipple as she goes, and I reel.

"Let me fuck you," I say. No, *beg*. There is no hiding the gravelly need in my voice, the desperation. My cock twitches between us, painfully hard, slicked from her mouth.

Josie cocks an eyebrow. "So soon? I need something first."

"I will give it." I try to bend down, but her vines keep me held, and I give her a breathless look of pleading. It sharpens, darkens. "Josie. Release me. Let me give you release."

"No. I don't think I will."

Her words take a beat to sink in.

No.

"Josie." My voice breaks, an ache I feel from the tip of my cock up to my shoulders down to the soles of my feet.

She backs up, grinning wickedly, and spreads her legs. Vines slither up her body, wrapping and contorting her until she is held aloft, legs splayed, cunt stretched wide for not only me, but the room as well. She is dripping already, her perfect lips glinting in the light, a small tuft of dark hair at the apex, and I want to bury my face in it, to lick and suck those folds, that clit, as she let me in the garden.

"Josie—"

She doesn't touch herself. Another vine disentangles itself and begins prodding at her entrance, and I make a disastrous crooning noise in the hollow of my throat. That vine will fuck her before I do, and I am equal parts infuriated and mesmerized.

The angle of her body lets me see her face thrown wide in ecstasy as the thick vine probs her cunt, then shifts up to swirl around her clit. She whines, needy and breathless, head throwing back and eyes shutting in bliss. The vine moves faster, tight, determined circles, and I watch her chest heave in quickening breaths, bottom lip caught between her teeth.

The room echoes with the throes of other passion being had, but I am transfixed on Josie's face, on the tightening of her cunt as the vine works her, building pleasure higher, her face reddening, lips breaking apart in a soundless cry. A shudder ripples out from her core, and I am so hard that I fear my cock will never again soften, not around her, not knowing the face she makes when she comes now.

"Josie," I beg again, limbs wound against the restraining vines, voice grating and hard.

Without opening her eyes, her fingers twitch.

The vines holding me release.

I stumble forward, a beast of primal drive, and reach her prone body, still displayed and spread, now for me, for my ministrations.

Hands coasting up her bare legs, I place myself at her entrance and sheath into her in one smooth thrust.

Josie cries out, eyes flashing open to lock on me.

I clamp my fingers into her hips and thrust again, drawing back nearly out and impaling myself into her, cock tip hitting the top of her womb in a flare of desire that careens me out into the abyss. She is so tight, so wet, so perfect in every way, and I am at her mercy in this moment, needing to serve her, to give her all of what I am capable.

Josie bends backwards, breasts jostling with each thrust as I fuck her, and I am driven by her building whines, the high pitched cries that tangle from her throat. But I have needs, too, and my need right now is to taste her—I grab her neck and haul her up to me and kiss her, lips tangling in a desperate crash that is more pain than pleasure.

"Josie," I whisper into her mouth. "Goddess, goddess—"

She clenches at the name. Her already tight cunt goes vise-like, and I explode without warning, orgasm ripping out of my body so forcefully I feel it in the back of my throat, a violent yank that has me crying out to the ceiling.

Josie picks up thrusting when my body shudders in stillness, dragging out a few last remnants and quakes, and then we are kissing again, lolling tongues and sweaty bodies ensnarled. My fingers wind into her hair, tugging, feeling, a transcendent, dreamlike state of bliss.

I lift Josie into my arms. I am done sharing the view of her, though the room has become more or less preoccupied with their own pursuits. Peppering kisses across her face and hair, I carry her up through the palace, but not to the suite she was given—I take us to my room, to my wide, empty bed, and there I pull us under a mound of blankets and sheets. She is limp with pleasure and so am I, but I am addicted to the taste of her, to the noises I can inspire from her lips. So as she lays in my bed, I trail my mouth down across her body, nipping and sucking and kissing every inch of her.

Six months at a time will not be long enough. I want her here, always, at my side.

How will I endure any time she is away?

How will I go about my days now knowing what has been absent for so very long?

A hand shakes my shoulder, rousing me from a deep, dreamless sleep.

I groan as I turn, already glaring at whoever would dare disturb me. Josie shifts next to me where she is curled into my chest, but she stays asleep, and that is my only solace as I roll to face Orfeas.

The look of concern on his face has me sitting up, trying to extricate myself from Josie without waking her. She stirs, twisting, eyes fluttering open in a brief moment of confusion before she recognizes me and where she is.

Her attention hits Orfeas, and she sits up, instantly alert.

"There had better be a good reason for this," I tell Orfeas.

His frown doesn't abate.

My stomach bottoms out.

"Unfortunately, there is," he says.

His eyes flash to Josie in question. I nod him along.

Orfeas sips in a breath, jaw setting, and presses on. "Very well, my lord. Sometime in the night, Zoticus escaped."

CHAPTER 13
JOSIE

oticus, my kidnapper, is free. And, from the bits and pieces I'm able to pick up from Hades's rushed conversation with Orfeas, it's clear that Zoticus has left the Underworld. They'd already sent parties out to search the realm they call home, and between the various demigods, there is enough power to confirm that Zoticus is not here.

Hades drops a kiss on my head, one that speaks of longing but is also distracted. Orfeas steps out of the room to give us a little privacy.

"Does this change things?" I ask. The fear had been winding around my heart, tightening, a snake that threatened to squeeze hope out of me.

"Zoticus committed the crime, not you." Hades's voice is low and warm.

He tucks a lock of hair behind my ear, his fingers

lingering on my skin. I can tell that he's grateful for the new perspective I gave him. I can only imagine what would have happened before, if a demigod escaped the Underworld for a significant amount of time. The brief moment where he found me in the falls, when I was already so close to the links to the Ancient Greeks, was a minor infraction compared to completely disappearing from the realm. I wonder if Hades would have insisted upon a total lockdown before.

"I have to do what I can to find him," Hades tells me now. "He is a child of Zeus, and with all the pompous entitlement that comes with that."

I snort. Zeus's reputation has existed for millennia for a reason.

"If you need anything," he continues, "Agapi will help you."

Another kiss, this one full of promise and passion, and then he's gone, and I am alone in his bed.

I get dressed slowly, and as I struggle with the brooches that hold the robes together, there's a soft knock on the door. I open it, and Agapi steps inside. "I thought you could use some assistance," they say.

"Thanks." I hold the brooches out to them, and they easily affix it to the white cloth, then sweep my hair over my shoulder.

"Perfect," Agapi says. They turn me around,

giving me a look. "Perfect," they say again, voice dropping.

I should be . . . I don't know, embarrassed, I suppose. After all, Agapi was there, with Orfeas. I saw them, my eyes heavy-lidded with sex-satisfied lust, as Hades carried me up here, I saw them fucking.

Not fucking. Making love.

But they—we—were all doing that last night. It wasn't truly an orgy, at least not for me, as I had no intention of sharing my body with anyone other than Hades. But for a moment, the entire feast hall feasted on nothing but each others' bodies.

Agapi smiles at me, a knowing twinkle in their eye. I can't be embarrassed; my body physically doesn't flush or react in any way other than to share Agapi's smile. Is it weird that everyone being in the same room, watching and playing together, has brought us all closer? I don't know . . . but I do know that Agapi seems like more of a friend than any of the people I left on the research trip with. Did the professor even notice when I went missing?

I flinch, thinking about the ramifications of how I've been here for so long already. *Someone* in the group had to have noticed I disappeared. They would have contacted my mother or Dr. Phillips. I may not have real friends on the trip to Greece with me, but I did have them back home. And they've got to be worried.

"Agapi," I say, urgency strangling my voice. "Hades told me that I would be able to communicate with my mother. I know that Zoticus escaping his prison is a top priority, but is there a way I can . . . "

My voice trails off at Agapi's frown. "Hades said you could communicate with a goddess?"

"My *mother*," I say. She is my mother first, not a goddess.

"I cannot bring you to the over world to meet with her," Agapi starts, "but if Hades said it was okay, then we could communicate with her by some of the old ways."

"I don't suppose there's a cell phone signal in the Underworld."

Agapi snorts. "No, but there is fire."

———

Agapi brings me to a different room in the palatial complex. Onyx, not marble, lines the walls, trimmed in shining gold and etched with ancient Greek meander patterns. Huge hearths have been built along one wall, and towering fires roared. Despite the wall of flame, it's neither hot nor smoky in the room.

A huge pedestal with a basin atop it stands in the center of the room. Agapi leads me to it, and I see the black stone basin is filled with shining, white salt.

"Allomancy," Agapi tells me, dipping their hand into the salt and letting the white crystals drift through their fingers, raining back into the basin. "The fires were made by Hecate herself."

Hecate, goddess of witchcraft. "She's now behind the River Lethe?" I ask, frowning. She had not seemed like a bad goddess. Unlike Zeus, Poseidon, or even the original Hades, Hecate had kept it in her own pants. And while Athena, Aphrodite, and Hera were well known to get vengeance on mortals, Hecate had been a quiet goddess, worshiped primarily by women.

"Perhaps we shall see some change in the future," Agapi says in a low voice. We're the only ones in the vast onyx hall, but they still speak in a whisper. "I think your presence here may mark a change. Demeter, too. Proving a goddess can exist without harming mortals *and* without the chains of the forgetting waters to keep her in check . . . it's a good start."

They reach out for me, their hand still salty as they grip my wrist. "I want you to know—Zoticus is the exception, not the rule. Hades is not a cruel dictator. We have all lived in fear that our unchecked power could cause undue harm. You have brought us all hope, Josie. We thank you for that."

I don't know what to say, so I just pull Agapi into a hug. I came to Greece to find temples and ruins, and instead I found demigods and the Underworld. But while I love Earth, I'm starting to think that a place like this may become a home, too.

Agapi straightens. "I'll give you privacy to speak with your mother. Meanwhile, to contact her with allomancy, simply throw the salt into the flames and speak her name. Her true name."

Demeter.

It's hard to think of my mother, Deana Granat, as Demeter.

But I nod to Agapi, and they leave me in the vast onyx room alone. I scoop up a handful of salt, my fingers wrapping into a fist around the white crystals, and tread softly to the center fire.

"Demeter," I say loudly, thinking of home as I throw the salt into the fire.

The flame shifts from yellow-orange to blue-white. I see flashes of images I can barely hold onto, flickering in the fire—the bell tower at the university, my apartment building, Maya's Victorian-house-turned-cafe. There's my mother's bakery; there's the home where I grew up.

But where is Mom?

"*Demeter,*" I say again, grabbing another fistful of salt. I focus not on location this time, but on Mom.

The flames don't show me my home town. The mountain range . . . I recognize it.

Greece.

The flames flicker down the path I took with the research group, down to the falls, past them to a building I don't know. It's old but serviceable; I guess it's the refuge where the research group was heading for the first night of the hike.

Inside, I see my mother, her hair bound by a bright yellow scarf.

"Mom!" I shout, unable to help myself.

Mom turns around, eyes widening in shock. "Josie?" Her gaze flicks around; I wonder what it looks like to her. She appears to me to be almost a flickering ghost in the fire, a cross between a science fiction hologram and something straight out of a fantasy novel. "Where are you?" my mother shouts, her big eyes focused right on me.

"Where am I? Where are *you?*"

"Greece," she says. "I got the call that you went missing."

And she boarded a plane right to me. Of course she did. My mother would do nothing less.

"I'm fine," I tell her. I can see her a little clearer now. She's in something like a kitchen—there's a big oven behind her, and she's standing in front of a table. I take a deep breath, preparing myself for what I know needs to be said. "I'm in the Underworld," I tell her. "The real Underworld."

Mom curses, but she doesn't look surprised. I push my luck and add, "And I know . . . I know the truth, Demeter."

"I'm your mother first, not a goddess."

I can only see her face and a bit of her neck and shoulders in the flames. She looks like she's kneading bread, her whole body engaged in the action of wrestling with unruly dough.

"You're not very surprised," I say.

"To be honest, I knew this was coming," Mom says. She glances up at me, and I see emotion in her eyes. "But . . . Josie, how could you do this to me?"

"Me, do something to you?" My voice is rising into a shout, but I don't care. "Mom, you lied to me my whole life."

"To protect you."

"From what?"

"From imprisonment!" Mom's shouting too. "And look what happened. The minute you leave my protection, you're in the Underworld." Emotions war on her face, anger and fear and something else, something I can't read.

This is her worst fear. Not, I realize now, me

growing up and getting independence from her. But me slipping through her fingers, to a place where she cannot reach me.

"Why didn't you tell me the truth?" I say, unable to hold back my emotion.

"Josie, my love, what good would it do?" Mom heaves herself at the bread dough, both arms pushing down against something I cannot see. Punching down sourdough, I suppose. I almost snort —how did I not see that Mom was the goddess of the grain? She literally made an entire business around the idea of a bountiful harvest, and even when she's in another country chasing after her missing daughter, her stress relief is baking.

"I was able to keep you safe as long as I kept you hidden. You're in the one spot I wanted to protect you from. You're in a prison. And I don't—" Mom punches down, taking her wrath out on the dough. "I don't know how to save you. I can't go there. You're a demigod; they won't torture you as they would me. Have you seen the River Lethe? The current Hades will force me to drink the water, force me to lose my own mind, lost in an eternal state of ignorant bliss, and I. Will. Not."

Mom punctuates every word with another punch at the dough.

"It's not like that any more," I say. "I've met the

Hades." I'm glad Mom's focus is a little off right now. It's one thing to have been in a room full of fucking demigods with Agapi, and another thing *entirely* to mention that to my *mother.* "Anyway," I say, clearing my throat. "This Hades is different. He's going to let you remain free."

Mom looks up at me through the flames. I can see her snarling distaste for Hades painted on her face, but there's also a little of that overbearing motherly look that I've grown to hate. She makes me feel like a child sometimes, and I don't appreciate it.

"You think your Hades is different?" Mom sneers. "Then why did he send one of his minions to come and capture me?"

She heaves up, and the picture in the flames shows me that Mom hadn't been kneading and punching bread dough.

Zoticus is a mangled, bloody mess in her hands. Mom has kicked his ass nine ways to Sunday. And from the look in her eyes, she's not done yet.

CHAPTER 14
HADES

My council is gathered in a meeting chamber, seated at a long table, arguing over one another.

"How did this happen?"

"Who was on duty? How did he escape?"

"No guards were unconscious, but keys were missing—it is likely we have a traitor in our midst who assisted him—"

At my entrance, their voices lower, attention pivoting to me.

In front of me, Orfeas drops into a seat at what will be my right hand once I join the head of the table. His face is red, jaw set with fury. If there is a guard who helped Zoticus escape, that person is under Orfeas's command, and I know he feels the failure on his shoulders.

Time for dealing with that will come later.

"What do we know of Zoticus's location?" I demand of the room.

A demigod at the far end, a descendant of Hermes, stands. "He has not gone far—he is on Earth," she says, holding an orb in her hands. She stares down into it, her eyes washing white. "He is—"

She stops. Her mouth dips open, shock twisting her brows.

"He is what?" I push, letting aggravation tinge my voice.

She looks up at me, the white of magic clearing from her eyes. "He is with . . . Demeter? But that cannot be right." A pause. "Can it?"

The room looks at me.

And my gut sinks.

Josie's arrival, her connection to Demeter, and now Zoticus's betrayal. It is all too convenient. Too irresistibly stacked together.

But Demeter would not be conspiring with Zoticus? To what end?

Josie is not a part of this.

She is *not*.

I need to speak with her. Now.

I have not yet taken a seat, and so I pivot for the door again. "I will take care of this."

Orfeas alone shoves up and races after me. We find Agapi, who directs us to a chamber I have never had cause to use, one with a wall of hearths filled with flames that allows communication with those on Earth, not dissimilar to the orb Hermes's descendant just used.

"You allowed her to speak to her mother?" I snap at Agapi.

Agapi gives me a flat look. "You yourself said it was all right, didn't you?"

I did. But something is happening, pieces connecting that I cannot make sense of—if Josie's mother is endangering her . . .

I shove into the chamber.

And see a mound of blue flame on the far wall of the room. Within the sparking, writhing fire is a face I have seen only in scrolls and engravings: Demeter.

At the base of the cauldron, Josie stands with her hands over her mouth.

Some of my worry eases at the sight of her still here. I don't know what I feared—that she had run off? That she was part of Zoticus's plot all along? What *is* his plot, though, beyond escaping for his own ends?

Why does this feel as though the first few pebbles preceding a landslide?

The image in the flames shifts.

Zoticus is there, with Demeter, bloody and beaten and nearly unconscious.

I charge across the room.

Josie hears my approach and turns. Her face lights up at the sight of me, and any thought I might have had about her betraying me vanishes. That is honest, pure delight to see me. It crashes over me in relief—and then immediately sours to concern.

She is delighted to see *me*. Me, the lord of the Underworld. The one who is forced to upend her life, bound by an ancient duty that I have never hated more than I do now.

But she reaches for me, and I cannot help but take her into my arms.

The image in the flames twists back to show Demeter's face fully.

She is *livid*.

"Get your hands," she barks, "off my daughter."

"Mom—" Josie starts.

I glare up at the fire. "Explain why you are in possession of my prisoner."

Demeter's lip curls. Her arm twitches, and Zoticus makes a pained cry. I fight a small grin of satisfaction.

Well, at least she isn't conspiring with him.

"Your *spy*, you mean," Demeter says.

"I did not send him after you. He escaped my

hold—and ran to *you*. I should very much like to know *why*."

Josie twists in my arms, looking up at me with a frown. This is my role, though. King and leader and oftentimes the one who must do what will bring blame and scorn. In this moment, it means meeting Demeter's energy with the same sort of distrust—even if she is not allied with Zoticus, she is still breaking the largest rule we live by in evading imprisonment here. I must treat her with nothing short of disdain.

Another punch I cannot see, the flames showing only Demeter's face.

"This one," Demeter says, and breaks for another strike. "Claimed to be here to seek my aid. What clever ruse did you conjure with him to get me off guard? As though I would fall for any of your puny tricks—"

"I did not send him," I say again, as firmly as I can.

"Mom—listen to him!" Josie interjects. "That guy is the reason I'm here at all. He abducted me from a pool in the mountains."

"In *Greece*, where you shouldn't have been at all!" Demeter wails on Zoticus, venting her frustration on him. "If you had listened to me, Josie—if you had *stayed*, none of this would have—"

"But it did," Josie says, her voice shaking, just a little. "It did happen. And I swear, Zoticus wasn't sent there by Hades, Mom."

"What did he say to you?" I try. "What did he say exactly?"

Demeter hesitates, still fuming, and glares at me through the flame. "That he needed my assistance to return all gods to their rightful place." She scoffs. "I know well what that means, and if you think I will ever willingly come to the Underworld only to be imprisoned and drugged by the Lethe—"

A sinking pit opens in my chest.

Behind me, Orfeas makes a choked grunt. "Return all gods to their rightful place?" he echoes.

I step forward, uncoiling my arm from Josie, fixated on the flame in a sudden pull like hypnosis.

"Let me speak to Zoticus," I say. Then I add, with a bow of my head. "Please, Goddess."

It stuns Demeter as much as it does Josie, next to me. The two of them are identical in shock, eyes wide, lips parted.

Demeter gathers herself first. She doesn't respond, but the flame shifts, and I see Zoticus's face fill the screen. He is bruised and bloodied, one eye swollen shut, lip cracked and dripping red down his chin.

He sneers at me. "Fuck off, *my lord.*"

"What have you been doing?" I ask, dread welling, welling.

Return all gods to their rightful place.

He wouldn't. He wouldn't be so stupid.

But I remember the way Zoticus was caught swimming in the Mnemosyne, nearly outside our bounds.

And I remember the way Hermes tried to escape. The way he tried, over and over, and it grated on me then, but now it feels pointed.

Why did Hermes try to cross the Lethe? None of the gods has ever tried before, not under my other ancestors. I brushed it off as a fluke and reinforced the guards.

"Hermes attempting to cross the river wasn't a fluke, was it?" I ask.

Zoticus's scowl warps into a feral grin. "You can't see what's happening right under your nose, Hades. And *that's* why it'll be your reign that goes down in history as proof of Hades's weakness and stupidity. Because you are the embodiment of it all."

Josie flinches at my side. "Shut up," she snaps.

Her visceral reaction, protectiveness, is the only thing that keeps me grounded.

Because Zoticus is right.

Zoticus laughs, the noise scratching on his throat. "Go and see for yourself. It's already started." He snaps a look up at Demeter—I don't miss that it's laced with actual fear. Good. "Your help would've been a boon, but we don't need a traitor goddess who let her siblings lie in torture and fog while she walked Earth *free*. We don't need *any of you*. And you'll all soon regret letting the strongest beings in all of creation fester and writhe."

He looks back at me. And grins again.

"You'll get what's coming to you, Hades," he says, and it is a promise.

"What," I fight to keep my voice level, "did you do?"

Zoticus scowls. Blood drips into his good eye. "The gods are waking up. *My lord*. You didn't think the powers of the Lethe would hold forever, did you? All they needed was a push. A few drops of the Mnemosyne in their food, in their drink. Now—" He spits into the flame, as though it could strike my face. "They'll be almost at your doorstep."

Horror fizzles through me, a hot, determined lightning strike.

He's stalling me.

This has been part ruse.

I whirl, and Josie is there, grabbing my arm immediately, and I unconsciously cling to her, unable to brush away how much more centered she makes me, how her very presence is a burst of calm.

"Mom!" Josie calls over her shoulder. "Don't let him go!"

"Wasn't planning on it," Demeter returns. There's a heavy thud, and I have to believe Zoticus is now unconscious.

I twist once more, to look at Demeter in the flame.

Her eyes connect with mine.

"Thank you," is all I say. No promise to come after her. No reprimand for the rule she broke.

She blinks away a pulse of surprise and nods at me.

My eyes go to Orfeas.

"We need to get to the river," I say, shaking. "Now."

CHAPTER 15
JOSIE

We all—me, Hades, Orfeas, Agapi—rush outside, Hades in the lead, dragging me by the hand through a labyrinth of passages that deposits us on a small platform right at the bank of the River Lethe.

Over the waters, on the other bank of the river, there are the gods.

I need no introduction. It is obvious who they are, not just because I've been a scholar of Ancient Greek mythology, but because the gods are so well known, even today.

At the head, there is Zeus. Huge and hulking, with a cocky smirk as he stares right across the water to Hades. He doesn't have his trademark lightning bolt, but I suspect that's just because he's nowhere near a sky from which he can call one down. I doubt he needs it. His fist is the size of a head.

I think of every legend I know of Zeus, most of them revolving around what a cruel, raping asshole he is. Near him, a lithe woman flicks her hair, golden eyes flashing. Hera. A goddess of motherhood, but a tormenter to the women Zeus raped, rabidly jealous and willing to ruin families to vent her rage.

A shock washes over me—these are my aunts and uncles across the river, brothers and sisters to my mother, Demeter. Not all of them have as cruel reputations as the King of the Gods, but many of them toyed with human lives, gambled with them as if they were chess pieces they could sacrifice in an amusing game.

I don't see Hades—the original, the namesake of my Hades. Among the pantheon, there are some missing. Killed? I don't think so. I don't think it's possible. But there are some more, like my mother, who must have gone into hiding—either here, or in some place on their side of the Underworld. And others hang back. There's a winged god I think must be Eros, who sits in the distance, head in his hands, a beautiful woman comforting him. Athena, goddess of wisdom and war, should be at her father's side, but she's not, the grey-eyed goddess watches from afar, frowning. Not all the gods agree with Zeus's hostile takeover.

Some learned from their imprisonment.

But they are also too afraid, I think, to fight back. They aren't going to aid Zeus, but nor will they stop him. They likely recall the old stories . . . I shake my head. No, they *lived* the old stories. Zeus took down Kronos, a Titan. These gods are afraid of him.

I frown.

These gods think my Hades will fail.

"Call the soldiers," Hades mutters, and Orfeas goes running. Agapi moves to stand at Hades's left side. I shift closer to his right.

"Children!" Zeus mocks, his voice booming so much that the cave walls shudder. "You are the weaker shades of our virile days, and you thought you could leave us trapped?"

"You do not deserve your freedom," Hades shouts back. "And you know it." His eyes scan the shore, but also go further back, to the gods and goddesses who are not attempting a revolution.

I know it's futile. Everyone's too afraid to stand up to Zeus.

"I have one faithful son," Zeus says. "Where is he? Zoticus?"

"Sorry!" I call. "My mom's kicking his ass right now."

Zeus, for the first time, notices me. His eyes rake over my body, and it feels like a violation, a threat. Hades shifts, one shoulder in front of me, instinct making him protective. "You will not cross that river," Hades growls.

In answer, Zeus breaks away from the crowd of gods, taking a step closer to the lapping waters of the River Lethe.

Behind us, the palace bursts with soldiers, armed demigods.

Children prepared to fight their parents.

It doesn't matter that these are adult children of gods and goddesses, I can see the fear in their stances.

But I also see the courage.

And I'm reminded of how Hades told me that the demigods all decided—for the good of humanity, they would protect Earth from the gods. Their mothers and, in some cases, fathers, were victims of the pantheon. They were partly human. They knew what was at stake. I've been kept in the dark by my mother, but it's clear that these soldiers have grappled with the idea of how cruel at least one of their parents were, and come to a conclusion like Hades did.

That if it took their own imprisonment, it was worth it to ensure their parent could not hurt others.

It breaks my heart, this impossible situation. All because the gods like Zeus felt themselves above any repercussions.

Rage burns hot inside me. I turn from the soldiers to the river.

Zeus has one foot in the Lethe. "My faithful son has been slowly releasing us from your hold," he says. "He may be half mortal, but he recognizes a true god. His father."

Hades is tense beside me, his eyes laser-focused on the way the River Lethe does not render Zeus harmless. Those waters are supposed to be a barrier, stronger than any wall, a way to ensure that Zeus, that no god, can cross over. Zeus should touch that river and forget himself, forget his rage, his intentions, his cruelty.

Ignorance is bliss.

But Zeus is unaffected by the river.

There is nothing to hold him back.

Fear ripples through the army of demigods gathered behind us.

"Josie," Hades says in a low voice. "I free you."

His eyes are on Zeus and the gods.

"What?" I ask.

"I free you. Escape. Run away. Go to your mother, and then go back in hiding."

My mind grapples with what he's saying. And I realize:

He doesn't expect to win this battle.

Well, fuck that noise.

Across from us, more of the gods and goddesses stride forward, emboldened by the way Zeus is unharmed. If the river is no longer magically protecting us, then we don't need to run.

We need better walls.

I break free, marching forward. Hades tries to call my name, but my ears are buzzing with power. I drop to my knees in the soft, damp earth by the river, and I *pull*.

I pull with every ounce of my power. I reach deep inside—deep inside me, deep inside the earth, and I *scream* for the plants. I do not make a sound that any one can hear, I know that. But I call for them. The vines and thorns, the mighty trees and the stinging nettle and the poisonous fruits. I summon them *all*.

And they come.

Where once there was a river, there is now an impenetrable forest. Green and brown choke the area, spotted with bright blossoms of a few flowers and fruits. Not even a gnat could squeeze between the leaves, so tightly packed are all the plants.

And they writhe. The vines flick out, the thorns loose from stems, the sickening scent of poisonous blooms spray toward where the gods had been. I see —magically, in a sense that comes from the plants that arrived at my call—the gods retreating on the other side of the river. One of them—Apollo, that fucker—shoots a fiery blast at my plants, and I feel, viscerally, the pain of burnt leaves, scorched trunks. I strain with my fingers, shooting vines out to wrap around every appendage of the god I can. Tight, stinging cords wrap around his wrists, ankles, neck. They creep up his robes and find anything they can to squeeze and tear and rend.

From the other side of the wall of plants, I hear a scream of pain.

Excellent.

Hades rushes to me, helping me to stand. "That is . . . " He looks at the wall of plants, eyes wide.

I shudder as the gods sever the vines that held Apollo, the pain of the cuts felt inside me. "It won't last," I gasp.

CHAPTER 16
HADES

My Josie is incredible.

All of the demigods gathered around us gape at her undeniable display of power. I feel the wash of their awe, the hum of their amazement—and, more strongly, the flare of their hope.

But bursts of flame erupt from the other side of Josie's plant wall. A roar, a crash, and punctures of light rip through.

She cannot hold back the gods of Olympus forever.

Neither, it seems, can the River Lethe hold them any longer.

The only reason the original Hades was even able to restrain them was through trickery and luck. Now, what tools do I have?

None.

All the tools given me by my ancestors were merely to maintain the status quo. That the gods might escape was never even a consideration—and I see now that it should have been, we should have always prepared for the eventuality that our duty could not last forever.

"Hades—" Agapi is at my side, their face pinched and pale. Next to them Orfeas is the same.

And Josie.

Josie looks over her shoulder at me, her arms trembling with strain, her face peppered with sweat, eyes blazing and fierce.

They all look to me.

And I do not know what to do.

"Leave," is all I can think to say. "Josie will only hold them off for so long."

"What?" Orfeas rounds on me. "Leave—the Underworld?"

"Yes." My body turns to stone. Rigid and unyielding to prevent myself from feeling the terror that threatens to unravel me. "The gods will want above all vengeance. It will give you time to block the exits from the Underworld. Seek out Demeter— perhaps she knows of others who can help on Earth. Prepare for—"

"Hades." Orfeas grabs my arm. "Are you saying you're going to stay?"

My jaw sets.

Yes.

Yes, I am saying that.

"Josie." I step closer to her, put my hand on her shoulder, feel the strain of her wound muscles and the vibration of power coursing through her veins. "Can you sever your hold and leave the plant wall intact?"

Because if she cannot escape with Agapi and Orfeas and the rest . . .

She glares at me. "So you can stay and die? Fat chance."

My eyebrows go up.

Josie's focus drifts from me, to the river still separating us from the wrath of the gods. She glowers, flares her hands, and more vines sprout up.

"There has to be another way," she grumbles.

My chest hollows. I have, in one way or another, before I even knew I was consciously aching for it, been seeking *another way* all my life. When I was younger, and my father ruled the Underworld with just as much cruelty as the imprisoned gods, taking what he wanted and punishing all who resisted— when I became the king of the Underworld myself, and I saw how my friends longed for a life beyond this wretched cave.

"There is no other way," I tell her, and I force myself to feel the truth in those words, because if I believe for even a moment that there is hope, I will crumble. "Josie, when I tell you to run, you *run*. Get ready."

I start to turn to Orfeas, to have him gather the other demigods and prepare to retreat to the surface.

After centuries of existing in extended punishment, this is not how we should be returning to the surface.

We deserve better than this.

Don't we?

We are the blood of the very gods trying to break free in wrath and fury.

But how many centuries of our suffering would it take to wash away the sins of our ancestors?

"Orfeas—" My throat is thick, eyes hot—

"*No*," Josie barks. "Orfeas—do not listen to him. There's another way!"

"There is no other way, Josie," I say, and I let my words break, let her hear all the emotion I am barely restraining. "Please. I—"

"No, *listen*—there is another way." Josie stares up at me, beseeching, her face red, exertion starting to tire her. "What the original Hades set up—it never actually punished the gods, did it? They clearly didn't see the wrong in their actions, at least not the big players. Some of the lesser gods, they seem to have learned their lessons. They're not joining in this revolt. But Zeus and the ones like him . . . they don't care about their past cruelty. They learned nothing. So we need to do something to make them feel the brunt of their shittiness."

"I—"

She doesn't give me a chance to speak. "The Mnemosyne. I'm going to waterboard Zeus in the Mnemosyne."

I jerk back. Her words barely process in the second it takes her to snap her arms together with a brittle shout.

The vine wall contracts. Beyond it, there is a sharp cry, a bellow, and then a body is lifted, Zeus, bound in a cocoon of green and writhing tendrils.

Josie doesn't hesitate.

She shifts, feet digging into the soft earth on the river bank, and with a heave and a tremor, she turns and flings Zeus over the Lethe, past the courtyard of the palace, and plunges his whole body into the quiet waters of the Mnemosyne.

Everyone sees. The demigods, taut with fear. The gods, who pause in their railing against the plants to peer through the gap Josie leaves, watching with tense anticipation for what will develop. Their pause gives me hope; they are dependent on Zeus to lead them.

So what happens next will determine the fate for us all.

My mind reels as I watch the surface of the Mnemosyne bubble around Josie's vines. This river is one of knowledge, of truth. Both this and the Lethe were avoided by the gods when they ruled for very different reasons—the Lethe made them forget, and the Mnemosyne made them too aware.

Ignorance is bliss. The gods have been able to live without remorse because they had forgotten they did anything bad.

But the Mnemosyne?

It would force them to remember. The few drops Zoticus had been feeding the gods was enough for them to remember their power, but this, what Josie is doing?

She's forcing Zeus to remember it *all*.

The aftermath. The hate. The accusations.

She's forcing him to face his own guilt. To *live* it.

The answer has been flowing through the Underworld this whole time, hasn't it?

We kept the gods trapped by the wrong river.

And Josie was the only one to see that.

I hear a strangled cry come from her. She's

overused her powers, exhaustion overwhelming her.

I whirl to her, suddenly not caring what happens to Zeus, to the gods on the other side of the Lethe, or even to the demigods around me. The only thing that matters is the goddess at my side, who drops to her knees, fingers arched like claws, eyes ferocious and teeth bared.

"Josie," I whisper, kneeling down next to her. I touch her face, her shoulder, cup her jaw in my hand. "Josie—"

Her eyes flick to mine. A look like resignation passes over her face. We do not know what will happen when Zeus comes out of the water, but she cannot hold him for long.

"Hades," she says back to me, and then she dives into my arms, releasing her hold on her plants with a gasping cry, her body going limp with exhaustion as I claim her mouth in a brutal kiss.

If this is to be our end, then I will end it with her.

CHAPTER 17
JOSIE

The plants did not want to be pulled up through the Underworld, a place without sunlight. They did not want to go against their nature, turning into a wall or driving Zeus into the River Mnemosyne. They bent to my will, but it was . . . hard. As Hades grabs for me, I feel my hold falling, much like he makes my reservations fall, my fears, my doubts.

When I come up for air from his heady kiss, Hades keeps a hand on my back, supporting me.

The gods—the aggressive ones, Hera, Apollo, Dionysus, the ones like them—have their eyes glued to the banks of the Mnemosyne. Zeus couldn't be drowned, but he comes up sputtering, clawing at the silty mud, bedraggled.

He doesn't look like a god any more.

Zeus collapses in the mud, and Orfeas and some of the other soldiers rush forward, seizing him. He does not put up a fight. He is no more than a blubbering, sobbing mess.

Nothing like the consequences of your own actions to bite you in the ass.

I go over the stories I know about Zeus. Assuming they're true, the Mnemosyne just forced him to relive not just his own cruelly apathetic actions, taking what—and who—he wanted, but it also made him live with the knowledge of just how painful and hurtful his actions were.

How can you pretend to be a beloved god when you know you're feared, not worshiped?

Hades makes a subtle gesture behind my back, and I see more of the demigod soldiers peeling away, carefully crossing the Lethe on the vines Josie left as a bridge and seizing the aggressive gods.

"I won't be like him!" Hera screams, and I am not sure if she means that she won't act cruelly as Zeus had, or if she means she won't be reduced to a simpering, wailing nervous breakdown with legs, but it doesn't matter.

The gods who had been drunk on forgetfulness are now going to be forced to remember. To face what and who they are.

No walls will be needed to restrain a god or goddess trapped inside their own mind.

But, for good measure, I note that Zeus is being dragged down to the dungeons anyway.

"Come on," Hades murmurs in my ear. I did not realize I was *so* exhausted. He supports my whole weight with his arm, and when I stumble, he swoops down, scooping me up in his arms.

"I can walk," I protest, but I snuggle into his arms, sighing happily. His chest rumbles with a low chuckle.

Safe.

Hades pauses on the way back to the palace only to speak to someone—Agapi. They are prepared to handle the shift in the prison system. The gods that had lingered in the back are willing to help.

Zoticus's plan backfired, I think drowsily. He wanted to wake up the gods slowly, and he did. But some of them tasted their memories and realized why the original Hades had sacrificed everything to keep them trapped. The big players like Zeus were so used to turning their back on any guilt that they were able to maintain a semblance of pretense, but many— perhaps even most—of the gods and goddesses of old used their sips of the Mnemosyne to reassess the situation, weigh their pasts.

Things are going to change.

That's the thought that I hold on to as Hades carries me up into his chamber. Things are going to change. The River Lethe will no longer form a barrier to trap the gods of old. Some of them—and many of the demigods—are going to go up to Earth now. Undercover, yes, their powers hidden by mortals, but . . .

There will be freedom between the realms.

All sorts of things are going to change.

I bury my face into Hades's chest. I feel like I have barely had a chance to know him, barely had a chance to come to terms with the idea of being here, with him.

I was . . .

I wanted . . .

"Josie?" he murmurs, nuzzling my hair aside so he can drop a kiss on my neck.

I'm clinging to him, not a passive passenger in his arms. I'm gripping him so tightly that he can't let go.

I don't want this to end.

I realize that now. All that I've done, all that's changed . . . there will be no more ambassadorship here in the Underworld. No more trial run for my mother. With the gods freed from the barrier of the River Lethe and with their trial by Mnemosyne replacing imprisonment . . . the limitations on the Underworld are going to shift and fade.

"Is everything okay?" Hades asks me, concern creasing his brow.

You don't need me any more, I think. But instead, I say, "Do you want me?" I mean—to stay. To be here. With him.

But from the dark, eager spark in his eyes, I see that he takes my words in a different route.

"I *always* want you, Josie," Hades tells me. He lowers me gently onto the mattress, and I can see his arousal. "Always," he says again, his voice firm.

"Well, that's good," I say. I sit up in the bed, my robe slipping on my shoulder. "Because right now? I would very much like to be wanted."

Hades pins his arms down on either side of me, dropping his head to mine and devouring my lips with a kiss that leaves me breathless. When we break apart, I gasp for breath, and Hades's lips slide down my neck, over my exposed shoulder, quickly undoing the brooch that cinches my dress. White cloth flutters down, my breasts falling free.

I start to speak, but Hades is a man of action. Nothing more than gasps and moans escape my lips as Hades bends over my body, intent on showering me with kisses, licks, nips from his eager mouth. I fall back on the bed, my hair splaying around me, and Hades crawls over my body, his legs on either side of my hips, his muscle-corded arms pressed on either side of my body as his mouth teases first one nipple, then the next.

I squirm, the coil of desire winding within me. I tug at his robes. Ah, these Greeks. They knew how to make easy-access clothing. Who cares that they invented gears and perfected bronze? They also made robes that get me to Hades's cock quicker, and frankly, that's exactly the thing I appreciate right now.

Hades slips a hand behind my back, lifting me up so he can make a better feast of my breasts, his teeth grazing my nipple. My hands are free, though, and I wrap them around his shaft, relishing in the strange dichotomy of such a hard thing still velvety to the touch.

He groans against my nipple, his warm breath sliding over me. We don't speak—this is a dance we both know, both want. He shifts one knee between my legs, nudging me to open for him.

I do, angling my hips up, silently begging for release from this tight tension. Hades grabs his cock, guiding it to the very entrance of me. I'm dripping for him; he's eager for me—but rather than push into me, he glides, slow and languidly long, slipping into my body and gently stretching me wide, wider. He fills me up, pushing all the way inside me, and I throw my head back, gasping, unable to fully grasp just how *good* it feels.

I'm so tight around him, and when I squeeze my inner walls, I know he can feel it. He glides out, my body already craving him, the sheer *satisfaction* of him filling me up again as he pushes back in, making my body melt around him.

We fall into a luxurious rhythm, our bodies moving with lithe, liquid grace, every time he pulls away, my hips rise up to meet him entering again. Sweat sheens our bodies, glistening.

But even as the heat of the moment sinks into our bodies, my need for release draws keening sounds from my lips. My hips rise quicker, my cunt clutches at his cock, my whole being begs for him, for his touch, his release. His hard cock grinds into that sensitive spot inside me, shattering my senses. Hades clutches both my hips, his fingers almost painful but grounding me to this moment, that spot, the place where he stretches me and fills me.

My legs go around his waist, my heels pushing him harder into me. My whole back half is off the bed, my head thrashing on the covers, my fists bunching in the cloth. My lips beg him, over and over again, *please, please, Hades, please.*

And one of his lands lets go of me, his thumb

swirling over my hard, aching clit, and I scream his name, my mind spins out in a fog of passion, my whole body shudders and pulses as I come apart at his touch.

CHAPTER 18
HADES

feel Josie come apart on my cock, and it is everything I can do to hold back my own release as she shudders and writhes beneath me.

"You are a miracle, Josie," I tell her, peppering kisses over her hair as I plunge in and out of her. Her crooning cry of orgasm piques into a shrill wail, her oversensitive cunt spasming around my iron-hard cock as I demand more sensation from her, more pleasure, dragging out the last ripples of her orgasm. "You are sunshine and life and beauty. Do you know what you have done for me, for my people? I worship you, Josie, worship you as you should be revered—you are perfect, my Josie—"

I come apart on her name, thrusting deep into her body, hitting a spot that makes her buck and shiver and those vibrations rip my body apart.

In more ways than one.

Everything I said is true.

She is the brightest source of goodness I have ever known. She saved not only me, but all of the demigods here. She came to our world and upended it in the best way possible, and she is perfection, utterly.

And perfection has no place in the Underworld.

She is destined for more than being here, than being lashed to my duties.

She belongs in the sun.

She belongs to forces greater than I deserve.

———

Josie sleeps for a full day after, and it is no wonder, with her display of power. Her rest allows me time to devote myself to the restructuring taking place, and I am glad for it.

It is, shockingly, easier to deal with the reorganization of the whole of the Underworld than it is to think about what I must tell her when she wakes up.

With the help of my council, I set about ensuring that the worst of the offenders from across the Lethe is doused in the Mnemosyne just as Zeus was. They are then locked in the dungeon, where none even tries to escape, so assaulted by the horrors of their own actions that they almost willingly remain locked away.

The rest of the gods slowly begin to reemerge into the Underworld. They meet with their descendants, the demigods who have carried the burden of their punishment all these years. The original Hades, my ancestor, is unconscious, knocked to as close to death as an immortal can get by Zeus before he staged his attempted coup. Healers believe he will awaken—I am in no hurry to meet him, seeing the gatherings that take place among the other demigods and their ancestors.

Understanding is tentative. Anger spikes. Orfeas has his hands full soothing relations.

But all of them, all of them, wait with bated breath for the plans Agapi and I make.

We will open the doorway to Earth.

We will allow the demigods to leave, provided they are worthy and do not wreak havoc on mortals. And, over time, we may even allow the gods to leave as well—they are on far thinner ground, but I know we cannot keep them down here forever. No one can stay here forever.

Not even the souls who are destined to haunt these shores.

Josie is still asleep when I make my way to Asphodel Meadows, Agapi at my side. The specters do not stir at my presence; all that has happened, the justice had for them, and they do not know, cannot know, not the way they are stuck in the Lethe's abyss.

I have in my hands a goblet of water from the Mnemosyne. Agapi, next to me, carries another.

One specter drifts close to me. Her eyes lift, meet mine, and I know she sees me, recognizes me for who and what I am.

I set the goblet on the stone ground between us.

"You chose to be here once," I say to her, to the others who drift around me. "But perhaps you might choose a different sort of afterlife. A different sort of peace."

Agapi sets their goblet down as well and eyes me as I turn. They fall in step with me, and I can feel their gaze stay on the side of my face.

"What?" I ask, flicking my eyes to them.

They smile. "What sort of peace will you choose?"

The question rocks through me. Heady and poisonous and tempting.

"Watching others claim their peace is ending enough for me," I say.

Agapi gives me a flat look. "That's hardly enough, Hades. What peace do you choose for *yourself*?"

My mouth goes dry.

How can they ask me that? How can they look at

me, at all I have let happen, and believe that I am at all deserving of the peace that the rest of my people can now seek? I kept everyone here trapped. I was jailor and torturer.

I turn away, and continue on in silence.

Agapi and I reach the palace to Orfeas rushing down the steps towards us, his face pale.

I immediately go on alert. Agapi runs to him, takes his hand, but Orfeas shakes head, brushing off their concern.

"You have a visitor," Orfeas says to me. "Waiting for you in the throne room. Demeter."

—

I hold my shoulders level as I stop atop the dais and stare down at Josie's mother.

At her feet is Zoticus's prone form. He is bruised and bloodied still, as though Demeter has been using him as a punching bag to vent her frustration the past day.

"I believe this is yours," Demeter says and nudges Zoticus with her toe.

I nod at Orfeas, who sends soldiers to haul Zoticus away.

"You have my thanks," I say, forcing my eyes back to Demeter.

"I don't want your thanks," Demeter spits. "I want my daughter."

"And you shall have her, too."

Demeter's mouth is open, her body wound for an argument. But at my words, she stops, flinches like I struck her.

"I—you will hand her over to me?"

"Yes. My attendant is fetching her now." Agapi will explain to Josie what she will be walking into.

Demeter blinks at me, then scowls. "What game are you playing?"

I sink onto the edge of my throne, trying to maintain a regal bearing, but exhaustion is dragging me down. I have no more energy for games, of any kind.

"Josie does not belong down here," I say to the floor. "Few do, I have come to see. She is free to leave."

Demeter clears her throat. After a long pause, she grunts. "You've saved yourself a lot of trouble. Would that your predecessors had even half as much sense."

Yes. Would that they had.

Would that my father had not been as manic and cruel as the gods we kept imprisoned.

Would that the original Hades had realized that his plan, though bold, would do nothing to bring lasting change.

Before I can say anything, a voice comes from the doorway behind my throne.

"You don't think I belong here?"

I fly to my feet and turn.

Josie comes into the throne room slowly, her ivory gown dragging the onyx floor. Her eyes are fixed on me, full of confusion and sadness and a flicker of betrayal.

Betrayal? This is what she wants—to leave. This is what she deserves.

This is what I deserve.

My chest contracts, lungs stunted.

"Your mother has come to escort you home," I say to her. "You have my leave to go."

Josie stops a few feet away from me. Even this close, this far, I feel the heat of her body, the tension in her limbs; I can smell the sweetness of her skin, can taste her on my tongue.

But I stay in place. Hands fisted. I do not reach for her.

"What if I don't want to go?" she asks, a bite of fire in her voice.

I almost smile at the fight in my Josie.

But she is not my Josie.

She was never supposed to be.

"The Underworld is reopening to the mortal realm," I tell her. "Thanks to you. You have done more for my people than I can ever begin to repay—but I can start, of course, by giving you your freedom. You belong on Earth, Josie. You belong in the light."

"And you don't?"

My head cocks. "Of course not. I'm Hades."

It's so simple. Yet encompasses . . . everything.

I am the King of the Underworld. I am the sole bearer of burden—though now, the burden is in fixing so very many mistakes.

My place is down here, overseeing the transference of demigods to Earth, making sure they do not wreak untold havoc and enforcing punishment if they do.

Jailor and torturer in a different way, now.

"So you're just letting me go?" The fire in Josie's voice wavers. Her eyes go glassy, and it catches me oddly.

She cannot want to stay?

She cannot honestly believe she would deserve to be trapped down here, in the dark and the death? What cause could she possibly have to want to stay?

But I see it. I see it in the pulse of her eyebrows, the way she looks at me like I am the sun she so deserves.

My breath goes out.

I am unworthy of her in every way, and she is a

goddess more than any other. It is senseless that she could look at me like that.

She would realize my unworthiness all too soon, if she did stay for me. She would resent me for ever letting her stay.

I cannot let her.

I cannot let her drown down here with me.

My eyes go to Demeter because I cannot bear the emotion on Josie's face, the thud of longing that grows and grows in my heart.

"You have my thanks," I say again, and I clasp my arms against my spine as I turn my back on the woman I have come to love, impossibly, eyes blurring as I angle for the door.

CHAPTER 19
JOSIE

watch him go.

I watch him go, and he doesn't turn back.

Not once.

"Come on, Josie." Mom grabs my hand and gently pulls me away. The throne room empties as the few demigods who'd been here either follow Hades or disperse to their own tasks.

I stumble a few steps after my mother and then grind my feels into the marble floor, stopping her. I'm mad as hell, but not just at Hades for so easily and willingly giving me up.

Mom has a lot to answer for, too.

"What you did was wrong." I speak the words flatly.

To her credit, Mom meets my eyes and nods in agreement. "I see that now," she says. "Please understand, though, that I'm immortal. I have had daughters before you, and that has, perhaps, made me more protective of you now. The Fates seem to watch my bloodline . . . "

Well, that's definitely something we'll be unpacking later. For now, I say, "So—you're going to let up? Trust me to make my own decisions?"

Mom hesitates for the barest flicker of a moment, then nods, agreeing. "I love you," she whispers, her eyes liquid as she stares at me.

"I love you, too," I say, and I wrap my arms around her. Despite everything, she's my mother. And I can understand why she's done and said what she did. Now, however, I hope we can grow to be more trusting, more equals. It can't be hard for *any* mother to let her child go off alone, much less a mother who's a goddess who's lived for millennia.

"Everyone back home has been so worried," Mom murmurs in my hair without releasing me from the hug. "Dr. Phillips has called daily."

How long have I been gone? I disappeared from the research group, yes, but . . . how many days has it been?

"Time moves differently for the gods," Mom says, answering my unasked question.

"Oh my god, am I going to fail?" The words strike me before I can even make sense of them.

Mom chuckles and finally lets me go. "You're worried about a degree?"

"It's my *doctorate*, Mom, and I've been working on it for nearly a decade now!"

"I . . . spoke with Dr. Phillips. Unusual woman." Mom's brow creases, then she re-focuses on me. "You've been missing for a few weeks only. We pulled some strings, covered up your disappearance, made excuses to the research program."

Part of me feels pretty good about that—the research program had good people, even if they weren't *my* people, if that makes sense. And if Dr. Phillips is the one making excuses, at least my friends in the Study Group aren't going to be worried sick.

"You have loyal friends," Mom continues. "I caught one of them in your apartment, trying to cover for you before we knew you'd been taken."

"Cate?" I guess.

"No, this one was called Marie," Mom says. "She swore at me in Gaelic."

"Yeah." I grin. "That's Marie."

"They're good friends." Mom smiles at me, and it suddenly hits me that Mom doesn't really have friends. She has lots of people she works with, and she has lots of people who celebrate her—her charity is renowned. She's gotten the key to the city from the mayor, and there are so many glass awards and plaques that we keep some boxed up in the garage. She does a lot of good, helps a lot of people, runs a successful business . . .

But she doesn't have any friends.

She's been too scared, I realized. For both me and herself—if she drew too much attention, she would reveal her location to Hades and the Underworld. Now that the system is changing, maybe she won't be so afraid.

I see a glimmer of gold through the doorway. One of Apollo's children, a lithe woman with shining blonde hair that hangs down to her knees. Apollo could be sadistic in his competitions for fame, but he was also a god of music and healing. This daughter of his—she may bring joy to the world through song, or she may help invent new ways to cure diseases.

The gods—and their children, the demigods like me—can use their powers for good. It's another reason Hades should be proud of what he's doing, creating a scaled back, monitored allowance of magic back into the world.

At that thought, a pang of sorrow hits my chest.

Mom notices. "Come on, my love," she says, squeezing my hand. "Let's go home."

I follow after her a few steps. "Is there some magical portal or something?" I ask. "How did you get to Greece, anyway?"

Mom snorts. "I flew. First flight I could get. Economy."

"Oh."

"Did you expect something different?" Mom laughs at me. "We're supposed to be undercover goddesses, after all."

"I guess." I catch up to Mom as she picks up her pace. "But maybe we can upgrade for the return flight?"

———

Mom's snoring on the plane. She splurged for first class, and I'm grateful for the extra leg room and the glasses of champagne.

But even after three, I'm not tired at all.

I lift up the shade over the window by my seat. From this distance, I can see nothing but the dark night sky and some clouds below. The screen in front of me says that we're over the Atlantic now, heading in a graceful arc back to America.

My heart twists.

I have wanted all my life to be a doctor of history. I grew up with grand plans of exploring archeological digs and presenting new ideas at seminars and curating exhibits at museums. I found not just education but also a home at the university.

I had my eyes on the target for so long, that I didn't look around me at anything else. I was going to graduate—with honors—and start my career globe-hopping to new locations and uncovering the riches of the past.

I wanted that for so long, it was all I could see.

But now?

All I wanted was for Hades to ask me to stay.

CHAPTER 20
HADES

work.

Agapi sets up in-depth interviews all the demigods must undergo before they can leave. I oversee each of them, my council as well, and we deliberate the worthiness of our people to be trusted on Earth. Those who are chosen are given lessons in what to expect, how to behave, what to do or not do. Our priority is in protecting mortals, above all. We do not go out merely for our own pleasure; we go with the sole task of making the world better for mortals, as should have always been the calling of those with god blood.

We are privileged and will use that privilege to uplift others.

The interviews and deliberation is grueling, but that slog is distracting and consuming, and I am grateful for the exhaustion that stays my constant companion. It distracts me from the way I search every room I enter, a helpless swipe of my eyes, hoping against all odds that Josie did not leave. That she came back.

But no, of course she is never there. She left with her mother, back in the sunlit world where she belongs.

I work, and work, and sleep fitfully, if at all, and Agapi prepares the first group of demigods to head for the surface, arranging a massive parade through the streets of our city and up to an entrance that has since been carved out.

All the while, I feel Agapi's sympathetic eyes on me. I feel the way Orfeas opens his mouth and starts to speak whenever we are briefly alone, but thinks better of it and stays quiet. They avoid me, more than they have in the past when I have been in moods like this; and I think it is because they know the solution, and they know I know it as well, and their refusal to remind me of what I gave up only sinks me deeper into my depression.

I let her go.

I had to let her go.

But I am hollow now, adrift, and I do not know how long this ache will last.

And then, one day, a new arrival is standing in my throne room.

I sit in my throne—his throne—and stare at him, hands fisted on the armrests, eyebrows tugged low. I do not know what to expect of the original Hades. My people don't, either; Orfeas stands at attention in the shadows with a number of guards. Agapi is off to the side of my throne, eyes flicking between us, half wanting to offer refreshments, half waiting to run for cover.

He looks like me.

Features I have seen in every mirror. Features I saw in my father, too, and it makes me hate him and fear him with a familiar ferocity, and I realize it is the hate and fear I felt towards my father, yes, but also the hate and fear I feel for myself.

My chest clenches. Guilt and self-loathing and all the usual darkness, but I see it at a distance now. I see its origin.

I stand. Hades has his hands behind his back, a long black toga draped around him, and the moment I stand, before I can even speak, he kneels.

He *kneels*.

For me.

"I owe you my life," he tells me.

The room goes so quiet it feels turned into a vacuum, all sound and sensation deadened.

"We have no life," I say. "Gods do not live."

He looks up at me, head tipping. "I have been informed of what happened, and how you undid what came to be my greatest mistake."

"It was not my doing."

"Yes. Demeter's daughter. But you encouraged her. You, lord of the Underworld, allowed her to intervene, and have since set about righting my wrongs. I owe you a life."

I bristle. "We have no life," I say again, harder; I do not know why his words grate on me—

Hades stands. "I said *a* life. I owe you *a* life. Because I have kept my descendants imprisoned for far too long, and you especially deserve far more than you have been dealt."

I flinch back. My mouth goes dry.

"I have been as complicit in our fate as you," I manage. "I—"

"But when given the chance to correct it, you acted." Hades bows his head at me. "I am sorry for the weight I put on you. I am sorry for the duty I forced on you. Allow me to make recompense."

"How?" It cuts out of me, full of distrust, full of caution.

Full of . . . hope.

Hades looks up at me again. "Allow me to help begin the process of fixing my mistakes."

"He could oversee the transition like you do," Agapi cuts in. They step forward, eyes on me, a smile on their red lips. "He could serve as your mediator when you need it."

"My mediator?" I frown. "What are you talking about?"

"When you go to the surface," Agapi says with a shrug. "You'll need someone to be here, in your place. Who better than another Hades?"

My jaw goes slack. "I am not going to the surface."

Agapi's look goes briefly furious. I have never seen them furious. It stuns me, and honestly terrifies me, and I go silent as they step up the dais to stand next to me.

"Orfeas and I are going to the surface eventually," they tell me. "And we want you with us."

"I—" I stutter; I don't *stutter*. "I cannot leave. I don't deserve—"

"Oh, shut it, Hades," Agapi snaps. "Enough with your wallowing. You think you're the only one who feels guilty for maintaining the status quo all these years?"

"It was not your duty—it was mine, mine to—"

"It was *all* of our duties. Yes, you may have been the de facto King, but all of the demigods went along with the arrangement. No one tried to push back, until Zoticus, which is worse in so many ways. We let this continue to play out even though we knew the penance we were paying was not our own. Stop trying to take full credit for this mistake, Hades. You are letting everyone else go—but you aren't letting *yourself* go."

My focus dips from Agapi to Hades, still below the dais, watching patiently.

"We could trust him?" I hear myself ask. As though I am considering leaving.

I cannot.

I will not.

I—I don't—

But something has taken wings in my chest. It flutters and spasms and I am ignited from within at what potential I see now. Hope, hope is dangerous, hope is powerful, and I am losing my grip on all I am certain of.

Because Hades gives a small smile and bows his head again. "I will prove myself to you. To any you need. But I quite like this arrangement." He smiles at Agapi. "It will give you what you should have been given from the start, Hades. A life. A duty to yourself."

The breath knocks out of me in a rush.

Never have I considered a duty I might have to

myself. To my people, to the Underworld, to Earth even—but what do I owe myself?

I feel my awareness peel back, seeing me as I see Agapi, as I see Orfeas, as I see the other demigods under my command. Is it possible I am the same as them, at the root of it all? Is it possible I deserve the same thing we are setting up for them—freedom, growth, sunlight?

Is it possible I could have something of a life . . . with Josie?

At the thought of her, the winged hope in my chest bucks and I press my hand to my sternum, fighting for breath.

Absently, numbly, I nod.

"All right," I breathe into the impossibility. I find myself returning Hades smile, and all that hope in my chest fills me, head to toe, a cleansing wash like I have been submerged in the Mnemosyne, too.

CHAPTER 21
JOSIE

My graduation ceremony comes far more quickly than I'd ever thought possible. After waiting for my doctorate for . . . all my life, really, the idea that it's finally *here* is a little mind boggling.

My mother sits through the ceremony, a beaming smile on her face the whole time. Beside her is a new love, a woman she met at her bakery, and I'm as happy for the fact that Mom is willing to branch out and claim joy for herself as I am for the piece of paper Dr. Phillips hands me on stage.

Afterwards, of course, we party.

It's something of a tradition for everyone in the Study Group, no matter their age or graduation date, to meet at Maya's after a graduation. Maya is in high form tonight—my mother provided every baked good a girl could ever want, so Maya's working only as bartender, a role the gray-haired woman does with as much aplomb as any member of Coyote Ugly.

Dr. Phillips tips her glass at me as I walk by, then knocks back her whiskey. Like I said, *every* member of the Study Group is invited—even those who graduated decades ago. It's a party not to be missed.

"I can see why you liked college!" Mom says, her voice loud as the music in the usually quiet Victorian pumps up.

I grin at her. "You have my permission to go," I tell her.

Her shoulders sag in relief. Parties are *not* my mother's jam. But she pulls me to the front porch of the Victorian, the music dulled by the walls. The night is warm and refreshing, sparkling like champagne.

"What's wrong?" I ask. Because she wears the same pinched look she used to sport all the time, before she'd told me the truth.

The door behind us opens, and Mom's girlfriend pokes her head outside. Mom gives her an "I'm doing it now" look and waves at Leigh, who shoots me an unreadable expression before disappearing back into the party.

"Okay, for real, what's wrong?" I ask again, more urgency in my voice.

"I didn't mean to do this here and now." Regret weaves through Mom's words. "But Leigh told me I had to say something before tomorrow, and I think we're about done for the night, and . . . "

"What *is it?*" I demand.

"I didn't mean to snoop," Mom says finally. "But I am planning a trip with Leigh later this month, and when I pulled up my travel account, I saw . . . "

I groan. She'd seen that I'd already purchased tickets to return to Greece.

I can't help but snort, though. "This is a much different reaction than you would have given me before," I say. Before, Mom would have had no problem either snooping or confessing to snoop. And she would have banned me from travel without even attempting to broach the topic.

"You're not thinking of going back, are you?" Mom asks, worry furrowing her brow.

She doesn't mean back to Greece.

She means back to *him.*

"The Underworld is a prison for our kind," Mom continues. "And while this new, young Hades has offered to open it, there's every chance that his grand plans fail. That place has proven to be an impenetrable prison to even the strongest gods; if you got trapped there—"

"Mom, stop," I say, holding my hands up. "Hades

would never let me be imprisoned."

"He cannot guarantee your safety."

"No one can, god or not."

That makes her pause.

"Besides," I continue, using her shock to my advantage, "I know what I want."

"A world without a sun?" she asks in a low voice.

"Him."

Mom snorts. "No one is worth the risk of that place."

"He is," I say calmly.

"He let you go."

That's a low blow, and Mom knows it—I can tell she regrets saying that before the words are out of her mouth.

Hades *did* let me go. And I've not forgiven him for that . . . but I've also not given him a chance to ask for forgiveness.

"I've made my mind up," I tell my mother. "The whole point of living this life is to choose how I want to live. And I choose to give him a shot."

Mom opens her mouth to protest, but then closes it. She nods resolutely. "I don't trust him," she says. "But I trust you. And your heart."

She opens her arms, and I step into a hug, letting her wrap me up in her love as she did ever since I was a child.

Something changes in Mom's posture. She steps back before I expect her to. "Well," she says, an odd look in her eyes. "In that case, I'll leave you to it."

I'm confused, but Mom disappears back into the house before I can say anything. I don't follow her. I need a moment in the dark.

I turn.

And that's when I see him.

Hades stands at the bottom of the porch, looking up at me. From his expression, I know he just heard every word.

"I'm so sorry," he says immediately, striding up the stairs towards me. "I was thinking only about giving you your freedom. I wanted you to stay. I didn't 'let you go'--I mean, I did, it's just—"

"You came here?" I ask, interrupting him.

"For you."

"You left the Underworld?"

"For you."

"I didn't think you wanted me," I say.

Something breaks in his face; true horror. He was so focused on making sure I knew I could leave the Underworld that he entirely forgot to give me the option to stay.

"I will want you for eternity," Hades says. "And even if I have you for that long, it will not be enough."

CHAPTER 22
HADES

She wanted to stay.

I knew a part of her did. I had seen it in her eyes, and I was not fool enough not to think she would have stayed if I had asked her. But the knowledge that I would have kept her in my darkness was too much, too painful, and I see now my failures even here, stretching out before me.

I am done failing. I am done actively being my own sort of jailor.

Josie goes perfectly still as I rise up the steps of the porch, her eyes as equal a tether as the moon overhead.

And the *stars*.

Those are what I see now in Josie's eyes when I stop in front of her. Starlight and moonlight and sunlight, vivid and dimensional and hypnotic.

Agapi had wept when we'd first come to the surface. They'd sobbed and Orfeas had held them and we'd watched a sunrise.

But none of that beauty compares to the softness that encompasses Josie's face when I cup her cheek in my hand and rub my thumb across her jaw.

"I am sorry," I say again, I will apologize for eternity if she needs it. "I should have given you the choice. So I come now to give you that choice, and whatever your decision, I will respect it."

Because maybe she has changed her mind.

Maybe my expulsion of her from the Underworld turned her off of whatever we had.

My heart squeezes at the horrifying thought. But I stand strong, emboldened by the way she doesn't shy from my touch.

"You will return to the Underworld?" she breathes.

"Eventually. I am bound to it. But I will strive to spend time on Earth as well, to personally monitor the ways in which the demigods reorient themselves."

Josie exhales. She nods, like something was decided.

Then she closes the space between us and kisses me.

I heft my arms around her, lifting her to my body

instantly, keeping her close, needing her closer. The thump of music and laughter echoes from within this house, so I know we are not alone, but I am driven by the need to strip her from these clothes and have her on the porch itself.

"My Josie," I say into her mouth. I rock back, needing confirmation, needing to hear her say it. "You are mine, then?"

She makes a hum of consent.

"You realize what that means?" Dread fights to be felt against the rise of desire. "That binding yourself to me burdens you with responsibility as well?"

That makes her head tip. Not in fear, but in consideration. "What sort of responsibility?"

"I am the King of the Underworld."

"Yes?"

"So you would be my queen."

Her eyes go wide. Beautifully, openly wide.

"Your queen," she echoes. And when she smiles, my heart takes flight.

She does not shy from the title and what it means. She looks, if anything, as though she has been waiting for such a thing, as though all the roads of her life have brought her to this moment.

And maybe they have.

Maybe this is fate, weaving us together, bringing us to this space of joint bliss and perfection.

"My queen," I say again, and I kiss that promise into her lips, her cheek, her soft eyelids. "My queen. Mine."

EPILOGUE

Dr. Phillips stares at her black coffee spiked with chili powder. It at least woke her up through the hangover. She usually is more reserved at the graduation parties, but . . .

She had a lot to celebrate lately.

Her computer trills, and Dr. Phillips turns blearily to it. Incoming video conference call from Cassie, one of her former students, who'd started a fellowship in Cairo several months ago. Dr. Phillips opens the link.

"Cassie—I mean, Dr. Gamal—how are you?"

"Dr. Phillips?" Cassie peers at her through the screen. "Are you okay?"

Dr. Phillips holds up her full coffee cup. "Graduation was yesterday."

"Ah, graduation." Cassie smiles, clearly thinking fondly of her own graduation. Pale light streams through the window behind her, but it is artificial, Dr. Phillips knows. It is still nighttime in Egypt.

Dr. Phillips takes a sip of her coffee, winces, and then takes another. "So, how can I help you?"

Cassie leans forward, her face filling the screen. "You know about my . . . special research," she says.

The coffee cup hides Dr. Phillips's smile. "Mmm," she says, acknowledging the question.

"There's been a new development."

"Oh?"

Cassie nods.

"In searching for the Duat, I have located an . . . interesting papyrus scroll."

"Do you need help translating it?"

Cassie shakes her head in wonder. "One day, you'll have to tell me how you seem to know every ancient language there is. You're better at hieroglyphics than any of my colleagues, but I have yet to come across a language you don't know equally as well."

Dr. Phillips takes another sip of her coffee.

"Anyway," Cassie continues, "it's not about the translation. I've already figured that part out." She looks surreptitiously around, but Dr. Phillips can't tell what she's looking at from this side of the screen.

"I'm going to have to . . . go away for awhile, I think," Cassie tells Dr. Phillips in a lower voice. "This

. . . research . . . is taking me out of Cairo. But I've already risked my fellowship just to get the papyrus. You know I've wanted nothing more than to work in this museum my whole life, and I don't want to risk it, but. . ."

"You want to find the Duat."

Cassie nods.

Dr. Phillips can sympathize. Of all her students, Cassie has been the most focused, the most determined to see her dreams to fruition. But her dreams are twofold. She wanted the prestigious museum job —and she'd gotten it—but she also chased a legend. The Duat, the Egyptian version of the underworld, was a myth.

But Cassie is determined to find it.

She wants the safety of the job, but the adventures of a lifetime.

Dr. Phillips frowns. She doesn't know if Cassie truly can have both, but she is willing to help her.

"I could call in a favor to Dr. Mohammed," she tells Cassie. "Request you, personally, to do some privatized research for me. It's the height of tourist season, but . . . "

"He'll grant me a leave of absence if you request it," Cassie says eagerly, her face brightening in a smile.

"This time." There is a hint of warning to Dr.

Phillips's voice. She has already called in some favors, and it will be difficult for Cassie to keep walking this fine line between her dream career and her passion.

"I just need one more shot," Cassie says, full of confidence.

Dr. Phillips doesn't mention that Cassie has asked for "one more shot" more than once. She has followed more dead ends than any other student Dr. Phillips has guided. But she has never given up.

So Dr. Phillips won't either.

"I believe in you," she tells Cassie, and she means it. "Go find your Egyptian gods."

BONUS MATERIAL

We want to thank you so much for sharing in this adventure with us! This book has been a labor of love, and it's made better by sharing with readers like you. Our newsletter will always keep you up-to-date with the latest sexy releases, and signing up will get you a free short story! You can subscribe at rarebooks.substack.com

Please consider leaving a review—they help new writers more than almost anything else, and ensure that we can keep writing this series.

What's next in Gods & Monsters? Each story in the series will follow a different member of the Study Group as they discover how the gods, monsters, myths, and legends they read about in books are in reality. Every novel in this shared-world series is a sexy adventure you won't want to miss!

Our next story will feature a new heroine and a new god . . .

Never miss a thing at rarebooks.substack.com!

READ A SAMPLE OF APHRODITE & HEPHAESTUS

Natasha and Liza are always working on their next book!

In addition to the Gods & Monsters Series, Liza and Natasha co-wrote the Heroes & Villains Series, which is complete now, available in ebook or paperback. Sign up for our newsletter and get a free novella featuring a very sexy encounter plus access to loads more free stories and bonuses.

Liza and Natasha both also write their own separate stories as well—and we think you'd like Natasha's sexy retelling of *Aphrodite and Hephaestus*, another Ancient Greek story just waiting to be told in a new way! Although this story isn't a part of the Gods and Monsters world, we think you'll love it!

———

Before Persephone and Hades, there was . . .

APHRODITE AND HEPHAESTUS

THE GODDESS OF BEAUTY

The moment I come into existence, I'm a new toy in a mountain of bored gods. The god of war marks me as a conquest; others see me as theirs to use and touch. I have a purpose: to spread beauty and love to the mortals we watch over. But how can I do that when I'm cursed to be **the ultimate prize?**

So I run. Straight into **him.**

The only god who hasn't claimed me. The only one I want to.

THE GOD OF CRAFTSMANSHIP

My siblings destroy anything new. I will not let them touch her.

This goddess makes it too easy to forget that my family was right to ostracize me to the darkness of my forge. Even though someone as perfect as her shouldn't love a beast like me, she is beauty, and I am skill, and our collision is inevitable.

Together, we do the impossible: create love in this mountain of greed.

But anything new on Olympus is a target.

And now, we aren't just gods.

We are a threat.

———

The pinpoint of my existence whittled down to this god's lips on mine. His mouth held open for a singular beat, letting me explore him—a lick at his tongue, the taste of spice in him, heat and velvet.

And then he grabbed the back of my head and held me to him and devoured my mouth, ravenous gulps that drew from every build of anticipation that had sparked between us.

I arched up against him and that movement dragged my clit along his cock again.

He consumed the moan I made, the noise echoing down his throat.

"Use me, Aphrodite," he said into me. "Bring yourself to orgasm on my cock."

"You aren't going to— *we* aren't going to—"

"Let them watch you ride you me." His words were

caresses on my face as he trailed his lips to my ear. "Let them think we're fucking. That is all they will get. The sight of your face twisted in pleasure, the sounds you make. That alone is more than they deserve."

Relief had me moaning again, this time in fluttering, unhinged need. I was unable to get my lips to form anything beyond the action of kissing him. I couldn't stop, gravity mooring me to his body as I licked at the seam of his mouth and began to rock my hips.

His fingers clamped to me—one hand on my neck, one on the small of my back.

No demands came from the crowd. No cheers, no noise at all. We could have been alone, if not for their eyes on us, the tension of their stunned confusion.

They had never seen a consummation like this.

I fell into a rhythm, rolling my hips back, thrusting up, the glide of his cock parting my wet lips so my swollen clit slid up and down his velvet hardness with each cadenced rock. I expected the ecstasy of this contact to plateau, but every movement only spurred me to want more, to *need* more, in a rising cyclone of fire and vitality.

Hephaestus pressed his nose to the side of my face, gasping, sweat beading on his forehead, dampening his neck where I held him. Every part of him was wound muscles, restraining his own release.

When my body began to shake, it broke a whimper out of me.

He gripped me tighter, using his hands to pulse my body in the rocking motion I had created. I couldn't continue, the sensation building, building, my thighs aching and my body going limp, but he guided me through it, and my whimper rose to a careening whine.

My head dipped back, face sheened, eyes fluttering shut. His lips delved onto my neck, sucking and biting the skin there, and that gentle pierce of his teeth sent a ricochet of pain straight to my clit.

I came, a manic, wailing scream of ecstasy, nerves alighting, colors spewing across my eyes in riots of gold and starlight. My cunt throbbed, reaching, clenching, and I felt my wetness thoroughly drenching his cock as I rode the tremors of orgasm on his iron erection.

He held me to him, cradling the back of my neck where my head was thrown to the ceiling. His gasps of breath were taut with pain, blasts of heated exhale into the bend of my shoulder.

We didn't speak, couldn't, locked in this high together, the falling down from it more like a gradual slip into silken warmth.

My lips found his again, and the kiss now was slow, unhurried.

But his cock was still hard between my legs.

He hadn't come.

What colossal restraint he had—what beautiful, remarkable control—

"You," I whimpered into his mouth. "You—"

"Do not worry for me," he pleaded, and I kissed my way across his face, to the rounded veins in his forehead, the sweat droplets gathered on his hairline. "What do you need? Are you all right?"

I panted, unable to catch my breath, licking at the salt of his skin, wanting to devour him whole. "I need you to come inside me," I told him. "I need you to fall apart between my legs."

He *roared*.

Hephaestus surged up from the bed, keeping my legs clasped around him, his hard cock lodged between us.

"The wedding is done," he shouted to the room, and he marched us through the crowd, kicking aside chairs; someone toppled to the floor with a cry, but he didn't stop, the heft of his iron boots banging with every step.

I looped my arms around his neck and sucked the lobe of his ear into my mouth as he carried me through the halls of Olympus. He half ran, half stumbled at times, cursing softly and groaning my name in such a pleading tear that I almost felt bad for tormenting him.

But now that I could taste him at will, I never wanted to stop.

Now that my body had felt even a fraction of what his could bring out in me, I would have to be renamed as the goddess of his pleasure only—there was no beauty in the world more exquisite than this.

Keep reading! *Aphrodite and Hephaestus* **is available at all major retailers.**

ALSO READ

ABOUT THE AUTHORS

Liza Penn and Natasha Luxe are a pair of author friends with bestselling books under different names. They joined forces—like all the best superheroes do—for the greater good.

You can keep up with them at their newsletter. Located at rarebooks.substack.com, they often feature links to freebies and bonus material.

For more information about all their books and extra goodies for readers, check out their website at thepennandluxe.com.

www.ingramcontent.com/pod-product-compliance
Lightning Source LLC
Chambersburg PA
CBHW061520120726
48001CB00004B/1374